"And will I able to dazzle you?"

Leon's purring voice succeeded in making her flush.

"I'm sure you'd be able to dazzle anybody, if you put your mind to it," she answered acidly.

"Then why can't I convince you to marry me?" he asked, pulling her back against him. She could feel the length of him imprinted down her spine. She closed her eyes, trying to hang on to reality. Leon was doing this from need, not love, she told herself grimly, because he wanted something.

"Leon, if you mention marriage just once more...." Her face hardened. "I'm never going to marry you so you can get back your share of the château. Never!"

Twisting herself from his arms, she ran out of the room, slamming the door so savagely that the château seemed to shudder.

Joanna Mansell finds writing hard work but very addictive. When she's not bashing away at her typewriter, she's usually got her nose buried in a book. She also loves gardening and daydreaming, two pastimes that go together remarkably well. The ambition of this Essex-born author is to write books that people will enjoy reading.

Books by Joanna Mansell

HARLEQUIN ROMANCE
2836—THE NIGHT IS DARK
2866—SLEEPING TIGER

Black Diamond

Joanna Mansell

Harlequin Books

TORONTO • NEW YORK • LONDON
AMSTERDAM • PARIS • SYDNEY • HAMBURG
STOCKHOLM • ATHENS • TOKYO • MILAN

Original hardcover edition published in 1987
by Mills & Boon Limited

ISBN 0-373-02894-6

Harlequin Romance first edition March 1988

along to the auditions—and to her utter amazement, she had been one of the girls finally chosen.

Since then, it had been hard work, long hours, and the pay wasn't fabulous, but she had loved every minute of it. She had her own tiny—if cripplingly expensive—apartment, she had made lots of friends among the other girls, and she was really pleased with the way her life was going at the moment.

Maggie clattered into place behind her, gloomily clutching a feather.

'My costume's moulting,' she complained.

Jessica grinned. 'Just be grateful that you've only lost a feather. A couple of nights ago, Sue flung her arms out a bit too vigorously and her top popped right off!'

Maggie's eyebrows shot up.

'What on earth did she do?'

'Kept on dancing, of course,' answered Jessica calmly. 'You know what they say about the show must go on.' She gave her head-dress one last hitch. 'Come on, the music's starting. We'd better get into place.'

For the first number, they didn't have much to do. They were just a glittering and glamorous background for a couple of the main dancers, who performed an athletic routine that got the revue off to a blistering start. It was probably just as well, mused Jessica to herself. In this exotic but cumbersome costume, and wearing cripplingly high-heeled shoes, anything more than a few basic dance steps would have been just about impossible.

Since she only had to glide around the stage looking graceful, she usually grabbed the opportunity to relax for a couple of minutes, snatching a quick breather before it was time to leave the stage again and dash up to the dressing-room for the next costume change. Tonight, though, she couldn't seem to relax at all; in fact, she felt oddly on edge. With a small frown, she realised she had

been stiff and tense ever since she had first stepped on to
the stage. And it wasn't stage-fright, she was sure of that.
She still sometimes got a faint fluttering in her stomach
while she was waiting in the wings, but this wasn't
anything like that, it was——

It was as if someone was staring at her so intently that
they were somehow getting right through to her, she
realised with some surprise.

She drew in a faintly unsteady breath, then tried to
force herself to relax. Of course you're being stared at,
she told herself derisively. There are hundreds of people
out there in the audience, every one of them looking
straight at the stage. It would be pretty odd if you *didn't*
have the impression that you were being stared at.

But she still couldn't get rid of the rather unnerving
sensation that there was one gaze that was harder, more
forceful than all the rest, fixed directly on her with such
intensity that it was actually raising the hairs on the nape
of her neck and sending a tiny quiver right down to the
base of her spine.

When the number was finally over, she almost rushed
off the stage. The next few minutes were as chaotic as
always, with everyone scrambling out of one costume
and wriggling into the next, leaving Jessica with no time
to think of anything except getting into her own outfit.
The next routine included a South American samba, and
the dancers were festooned with plastic fruit and silk
flowers, with great pyramids of fruit balanced precariously on their heads.

'Over the top, but definitely colourful,' was Maggie's
verdict, and she hastily tucked a bunch of grapes into
place as she and Jessica breathlessly gathered in the
wings again, ready to samba their way back on to the
stage.

Jessica didn't answer. Her throat had gone oddly dry,

and quite suddenly she would have given anything not to have had to go back on that stage again. She hadn't the slightest idea why her nerves had suddenly gone to pieces like this, she just knew that she didn't want to stand under those blazing spotlights and feel him staring at her again, fixing her in that all-powerful gaze.

Him? she questioned herself silently. How could she be so sure it was a man? She didn't know. She didn't even particularly care. All she knew was that she definitely didn't want to experience that skin-prickling sensation again.

'That's our cue,' murmured Maggie, giving her a slight push, and Jessica found herself tottering out into the blaze of light. For the first few seconds, her brain and body just wouldn't function properly, her co-ordination was shot to pieces and she nearly got the steps wrong. And all the time she was tensely waiting for that creepy tingling to start crawling over the nape of her neck again, warning her that she was still being intently watched.

To her utter relief, it didn't happen. You see? she told herself with a first touch of impatience. The whole thing was just a stupid trick of your imagination. You're over-tired, that's all. A good night's sleep is what you need, then perhaps you'll forget all these daft fantasies about being watched by some laser-eyed stranger.

She got through the rest of the show without any problems. By the time she was trudging up to the dressing-room for the very last time, she had almost forgotten about the whole peculiar incident. Reaching the dressing-room, she kicked off the high-heeled shoes with a huge sigh of relief, then massaged her aching feet.

'Sue and I are going for a late supper at the café round the corner. Want to come with us?' invited Maggie.

'I don't think so,' answered Jessica, stifling a yawn. 'I'm really flaked out. There are a couple of loose straps I

want to sew on one of the costumes, then I think I'll just
crawl off home to bed.'

'Well, if you change your mind, you know where to
find us. Ready, Sue?'

Maggie and Sue left and, as the other girls got ready to
leave, Jessica slowly creamed off the heavy stage make-
up, seeing her own face slowly appearing from behind
the mask, her violet eyes looking larger than ever, and
her skin seeming startlingly pale without the bright
smudge of blusher along her cheekbones. Then she
loosened her hair from the tight knot on top of her head,
letting it fall in a mass of dark, tousled curls around her
shoulders.

'See you tomorrow, Jessica,' called out Janie over her
shoulder.

Janie was the last one to leave the dressing-room. As
she closed the door behind her, it went very quiet.
Although it was no less chaotic, thought Jessica wryly,
glancing round at the jumble of make-up, discarded
tights, hairpins and glitzy jewellery. Only the costumes
were meticulously hung on the rail provided, with a sheet
thrown over them to protect them from dust and dirt.
Hand-sewn and elaborately trimmed, they cost a small
fortune, and woe betide any dancer who seriously
damaged one!

Carefully lifting down the costume with the loose
straps, Jessica laid it on a chair, then searched for a
needle and cotton. She supposed she could have left it
until tomorrow, but she might have forgotten about it by
then and she definitely didn't want to have the same
embarrassing accident as Sue. Sue had carried it off with
great aplomb, dancing on confidently, her head held
high, as if completely oblivious to the fact that she was
naked to the waist. And why not? The audience probably
hadn't even noticed, they had already been dazzled by

the showgirls, who were chosen for their spectacular looks and bodies. What was so special about one more half-naked girl? Anyway, it was funny but Jessica knew that the audience often became fairly indifferent to the fact that a lot of the girls were wearing little more than a sequined G-string. They got caught up in the sheer spectacle of the revue with its fast-moving routines, the fantastic costumes and brilliant sets.

All the same, if *her* top came off during one of the more energetic numbers, Jessica was sure she would just turn bright scarlet and scuttle straight off the stage, clutching her hands in front of her. She wasn't particularly prudish—at least, she didn't think she was—but that kind of situation would definitely be more than she could cope with!

She began to sew quickly and neatly. The straps on her costumes often seemed to work loose. The tops were usually made of some fairly flimsy material, which didn't stand up too well to the strain her body put on them. Jessica grimaced. It was hard to believe she had been such a thin, gawky child. She was still slim, but during her teens she had suddenly shot up to her present height of five foot ten, and her body had developed fairly spectacular curves that set off her new height. It had put paid to her childish ambition of being a ballet dancer, of course: no one wanted a ballerina who towered over her partner every time she went up *en pointe*, but perhaps that hadn't been a bad thing. She wasn't at all sure that she had the temperament for all the relentless hard work and rigid discipline that ballet demanded. It had been Aunt Lettie who had suggested that she switch to modern dance, where height was a positive advantage.

Jessica stopped sewing for a moment, and her face softened. It had been two years since Aunt Lettie had died, and there were times when she still missed her with an aching intensity. By the time Jessica was six, both her parents had gone, and after that there had been just her and Aunt Lettie. And now Aunt Lettie was dead, and she was truly on her own, no family at all. Whenever she stopped to think about it, she always felt an agonising ache of pure loneliness—which was why she deliberately blocked it from her mind most of the time, fiercely concentrating on the present in a determined effort not to give way to self-pity.

She closed her eyes for a few seconds, suddenly feeling very tired and drained. A year ago, she had thought her loneliness was over. After she had met Steven, she had been so certain she had found someone who was going to share the rest of her life with her. Only that had been a mistake, a very bad mistake—and one that she had absolutely no intention of making again. All right, so she was lonely. Well, she could cope with that, and it really wasn't too bad as long as you worked hard and had some good friends——

Her thoughts started to drift away from her, and her eyes grew even more heavy. She really was tired, she thought to herself dozily. She ought to get back to her apartment, flop into bed and have a long, undisturbed sleep.

Only she was already dozing off, sprawled in the chair, her head resting on her arms. She made a half-hearted effort to wake herself up again, but then abandoned the attempt. It wouldn't hurt to nap for just a few minutes, perhaps it would give her enough energy to face the long walk back to her apartment——

Just seconds later, Jessica was peacefully asleep, her breathing quiet and even. And she didn't wake up again until her arm gave a small jerk, knocking a pot of make-up on to the floor with a loud clatter.

'What——?' she muttered confusedly, then she

blinked hard and remembered where she was. A quick glance at her watch made her groan. 'Damn, I didn't mean to sleep so long!' A little stiffly, she hauled herself to her feet; then, without any warning, she suddenly started to cough.

As the paroxysm slowly subsided, she rubbed the tears from her watering eyes and at last realised what she had been too half-asleep to notice before. The dressing-room seemed strangely hazy, and there was a sharp yet familiar smell drifting in the air.

Smoke! Alarm bells began to jangle very loudly inside her confused mind, her head shot up; and her eyes opened wide in sudden fear. Somewhere very close by, there was a fire!

As a burst of pure panic gripped her, she bolted over to the door and was just about to fling it open when vague memories of fire drills filtered back into her head. Opening doors could be highly dangerous when there was a fire. The sudden rush of oxygen could feed the flames, turning a minor fire into a blazing furnace.

Her hands shaking very badly now, Jessica gingerly turned the handle, somehow fighting back the almost overwhelming urge to yank it open and rush blindly out. Instead, very slowly, she eased the door open just a fraction so that she could peer through the crack to the corridor outside.

To her horror, she found the smoke was thicker there—much, much thicker! She could hardly see the top of the narrow staircase that led down to safety. And more smoke was swirling its way upwards even as she watched, snaking its way towards her.

Trembling almost uncontrollably, she shut the door tight again, then slumped against it as her legs went too weak to hold her up. What on earth should she do? Try and make a run for it down the narrow staircase? But what if she didn't make it, if the choking smoke filled her lungs and she passed out? She would just lie there until the flames caught up with her and——

Jessica shuddered violently as appallingly vivid pictures flashed through her mind. What was the alternative, though? To stay here in this still comparatively smoke-free dressing-room, and just pray that someone would come to the rescue in time? But no one knew she was here. The rest of the girls had all gone home ages ago, they would think the dressing-rooms were empty.

Her heart pounding frantically, she eased the door open again just an inch and was instantly horrified to see how much thicker the smoke had got since she had last looked. Pretty soon, she would have no choice at all. The smoke would come swirling through the cracks round the door, then it wouldn't be long before she wouldn't be able to breathe. She was already coughing spasmodically, and her throat and lungs felt frighteningly dry and prickly as she began to breathe in the deadly fumes.

Better to suffocate trying to escape than to die trapped here in this tiny dressing-room, she decided with a sudden flash of determination. Now that she had made the decision, she quickly drew in a couple of deep breaths, ready for her plunge into the smoke-filled, oxygen-starved air on the other side of the door. She was just about to launch herself on her frantic dash to safety when the door of the dressing-room was abruptly flung open, and a tall, dark shadow hurtled through, then towered over her.

Already terrified out of her wits, Jessica screamed with pure fear. He looked like the devil himself, appearing out of the smoke like an apparition straight from hell, gusts of smoke still swirling around him as he came towards her. His eyes were burning bright, and the dark, satanic lines of his face were vividly emphasised by a long, jagged scar than ran right along one cheekbone.

Going straight past her, he tore off the sheet that hung over the costume-rail, whipped through the costumes themselves, then finally dragged out a couple of long, red velvet cloaks that were used in a scene depicting an old-fashioned Christmas.

'Where's the sink?' he demanded in a harsh, curt voice.

Wordlessly, she pointed to the tiny, chipped sink which stood in the corner. She watched with horror as he turned the taps full on and plunged the heavy cloaks into the water. Ridiculously, she wanted to protest that the costumes were hideously expensive, that he shouldn't be treating them like that. Then one of the wet cloaks was flung over her head, she couldn't see or hear anything, and she certainly couldn't talk. All she was aware of was the hard arm and body that relentlessly propelled her forward, somehow keeping her upright as she stumbled along, almost carrying her when they finally reached the stairs.

Her head began to reel hopelessly as the lack of oxygen started to get to her, and her sore, aching lungs heaved in vain for air, but couldn't find any. She was dimly aware that they were still crashing their way down the stairs, but a hazy blackness was starting to swallow her up now; in just a few more seconds she was going to pass out completely, and in a way she was almost glad, this was like hell on earth and she didn't think she could stand it any longer——

Then unbelievably, miraculously, she found she could actually breathe again. She was coughing and retching, and nauseatingly dizzy, but air was finally getting into her starved lungs. Although she still couldn't see anything through her sore, streaming eyes, she was vaguely aware that someone was worriedly saying that they hadn't known she was there, that the girls didn't usually stay so late.

'It doesn't matter, I'll take care of her,' said a second, much grimmer voice, a voice which already sounded strangely familiar.

Jessica felt herself being lifted, and seconds later she was half sitting, half lying in a car. She was vaguely aware of the tang of leather breaking through the overpowering smell of smoke, then felt a sense of movement as the car gathered speed.

She didn't think they drove very far. Through eyes that were still sore and watering, she saw a blurred black shadow leaning over her and scooping her up again, then there was the rather pleasant sensation of human warmth pressing against her.

Another murmur of voices, then all was silent again. She was now lying on something soft, silky, and marvellously comfortable. Forcing her heavy eyes open, she blinked hard, and for a few moments had a clear view of the man looming over her.

Black hair, black brows, black eyes that glittered fiercely.

I was right, she thought woozily. I've been rescued by the devil! Then her stinging, aching eyes slid shut and she tumbled into the deep, dreamless sleep of utter exhaustion.

When she finally woke up again, she opened her eyes and was instantly dazzled by a blaze of sunshine streaming in through a large window. Feeling dazed and totally disorientated, she struggled to work out where she was, why she was lying on a huge, soft bed instead of her own rather hard mattress, and why she felt so headachey and lethargic.

Jessica turned her head slightly to the left, and her gaze instantly became fixed on the tall, dark silhouette emblazoned against the dazzling glare of the sunlit window. Screwing up her sore eyes, she tried to make out more details, but the bright glare defeated her. All she could see was that large and somehow threatening black shadow.

At last the shadow moved, out of the blinding sunshine and across to the patch of shade on the far side of the room. And as Jessica's eyes slowly began to adjust to the change of light, memories suddenly started to crash back into her mind and she sat up with a swift, sharp gasp.

The fire, the awful terror of that moment when she had realised she was trapped—the black figure who had hurtled into the dressing-room and dragged her to safety——

She relaxed a fraction as she realised that it was all over now, she was safe. Then, with growing curiosity, she let her gaze slide back to the man who had rescued her. Was this his apartment? Yes, she supposed that it had to be. But that meant she was lying in his bed, and for some reason she found that thought oddly disturbing.

She studied him from under lowered lashes. In the clear morning light, he looked a little less satanic—but only a little, she decided with a small twinge of unease. His eyes, his hair were still as black, and she hadn't imagined that wicked scar which slashed across one side of his face, marring what might otherwise have been rather awesomely perfect features. Nor had her terrified mind exaggerated his height, or the rather overwhelming presence of the man. She guessed he was in his early thirties, although it was difficult to be sure. His tanned skin was unlined, but those black eyes looked as if they had seen a whole lifetime of experience.

She was a little disconcerted to note that he seemed to

be studying her almost as intently as she was looking at
him. It was impossible to guess what lay behind that
black gaze, though; the darkness of his eyes hid all his
thoughts, all his secrets. And although a faint smile
touched the severe corners of his mouth, somehow it
wasn't a pleasant or friendly smile; in fact, it sent a tiny,
familiar tingle crawling over the nape of her neck.

And in that instant Jessica knew—she was absolutely
certain—that it was this man's dark gaze that she had felt
boring into her on stage last night, making her skin
prickle in precisely the same way it was right now. But
who was he? And why was he so very interested in her?

Before she could ask him, other questions started to
tumble into her mind, questions which seemed far more
important. She propped herself up against the soft
pillows and stared at him anxiously.

'The fire last night,' she croaked urgently, 'how bad
was it? Was anyone else hurt?'

'It was fairly extensive, but you were the only one
trapped inside the building,' he answered her, his
English perfect, his voice betraying only the slightest
trace of a French accent. 'It caused quite a lot of damage,
though. It will probably be several weeks before the
revue opens again.'

'Oh,' she muttered with a small frown, wondering
what she was going to do in the meantime. Would they go
on paying her wages until the revue reopened? And if
they didn't, what on earth would she live on? She had
better ring someone up straight away, try to find out what
was going on. She swung her legs over the side of the bed,
trying to ignore the heavy thumping in her aching head.
'Do you have a phone I can use?'

'You can use the phone later,' he replied curtly. 'First
of all, we've got some rather important things to discuss.'

Something in his tone made Jessica glance at him a

little edgily. 'Have we?' Then, rather late in the day, she remembered that she hadn't even thanked him yet for dragging her out of the smoke-filled theatre. 'You saved my life,' she told him, a note of warm gratitude creeping into her voice. 'I don't know what would have happened if you hadn't hauled me out of there——'

'You would have been suffocated by the smoke,' he interrupted curtly. Jessica was faintly alarmed to discover that his black gaze had gone unpleasantly cold. 'And if I had any sense, I'd have left you there and let it happen,' he added in a low undertone, abruptly turning away from her.

She stared at his broad back, hardly able to believe he had actually said such an awful thing. Was he just mad at her because he had had to risk his own life in order to drag her to safety? No, there was more to it than that, she was absolutely sure of it. Just look at the way this man set all of her nerves jangling! She decided it was time to try and find out exactly what was going on.

'How did you know I was trapped in that dressing-room?' she asked him bluntly.

He swung back to face her, his hard eyes fixing on her again with that same disconcerting coldness.

'Because I was waiting at the theatre door for you. When the fire started and you still hadn't come out, I knew you had to be in there somewhere. It took me longer than I expected to find you, though. That dressing-room was at the very top of the building, it was one of the very last places I tried.' His face darkened. 'What the hell were you doing, sitting up there while the building went up in flames all around you?' he demanded.

'I fell asleep,' she admitted sheepishly. 'When I woke up, the place was already full of smoke. I panicked, I didn't know what to do. I was just going to make a dash for safety when you came charging in.' Then she remembered something he had said previously. '*Why* were you waiting for me?' she asked curiously.

'Because I thought that it was about time we met, Mademoiselle Jessica Bryant.'

And at that, her nerves gave a hefty twitch.

'You know my name?'

'Oh, yes, I know your name,' he answered softly.

She stared at him suspiciously.

'And were you sitting in the audience during the opening number last night? Staring at me?' she challenged.

'I came in for a few minutes and watched the opening routine,' he agreed.

Jessica felt more and more uneasy.

'You seem to know an awful lot about me,' she said slowly, at last. 'But I don't know the first thing about you. I don't even know your name.'

'That's very easily remedied.' He gave a formal, rather mocking bow. 'I am Léon Castillon, Comte de Sévignac. And I also happen to be your stepbrother.'

CHAPTER TWO

JESSICA released a silent sigh of relief. There was no need to be worried, after all. This was just some simple mistake, Léon Castillon had got her mixed up with someone else.

'My name's certainly Jessica Bryant,' she agreed, almost cheerfully. 'But I suppose it's not a particularly uncommon name. And I'm definitely not the Jessica Bryant you're looking for. Sorry to disappoint you——'

'Oh, I'm not disappointed,' Léon Castillon told her evenly. 'Neither have I made a mistake. I've made very detailed enquiries about you. Would you like me to tell you something about yourself? Your father died when you were six, and after that you were raised by your Aunt Lettie. You had a good academic record at school, but dancing was always your main interest, although you had to switch to modern dance after you grew too tall for the ballet. Your Aunt Lettie died a couple of years ago, and since then you've been trying to make it as a dancer, but your career didn't really take off until you passed the audition for the revue. Your mother——'

Shocked that this stranger should know so much about her, Jessica jumped to her feet and glared at him furiously.

'Since you've obviously been prying into my past, you no doubt know that my parents were divorced when I was three years old. My mother went off, and I haven't seen her or heard from her since.'

She knew her voice sounded hard, but she couldn't help it; she was never going to be able to forgive her

21

mother for abandoning her so completely. It was a deeply buried hurt that had never healed, never would heal. And she fiercely resented this man for dragging all the old painful memories to the surface again.

Léon Castillon's black brows drew together in a brooding frown.

'I think you had better sit down,' he advised.

She was just about to tell him that she didn't *want* to sit down when something in his eyes warned her that perhaps it would be better to do as he had suggested. Disturbed and angry, she perched on the edge of the bed, her shoulders hunched tensely.

'Well, what's this all about?' she demanded. 'And how do you know so much about me?'

He gave a brief shrug. 'There's no easy way to tell you this, so I'll just give you the straight facts. Your mother was half-French—you probably know that. After her divorce, she returned to France, and a few months later she met my father. He had been a widower for several years, my own mother died when I was seven. Within a month of that first meeting, my father and your mother were married. The marriage lasted seventeen years, until your mother was killed by a hit-and-run driver. And that marriage makes you and I stepbrother and stepsister, Mademoiselle Jessica Bryant.'

Jessica was finding it hard to take any of it in, in fact she felt as if suddenly she couldn't even breathe. One fact shone through with starkly vivid clarity, though. Her mother was dead! She couldn't even hate her any more because her mother didn't exist, except as the shadowy memory of a three-year-old child.

She discovered she was shaking very badly. Seconds later, a glass was being held to her mouth and she smelt the sharp fumes of brandy.

'Drink this!' Léon ordered.

She wasn't in any state to argue with him. Instead, she obediently swallowed, then nearly choked as the strong spirit burned its way down her throat. It did the trick, though; the room slowly drifted back into focus and her brain started to function again. She was still shaking, but not so badly. If she kept her hands tightly clasped together, then Léon Castillon—*her stepbrother*—wouldn't be able to see the betraying tremors.

'You're certain—absolutely certain—that you've got the right person?' she muttered in a low, unsteady voice, still not quite able to believe it.

'I'm certain,' he assured her a trifle grimly. 'Your mother was Celestine Bryant. At least, she was until she married my father and became Celestine Castillon, Comtesse de Sévignac. She enjoyed having a title,' he added in a dark undertone.

From his tone, from his entire manner, Jessica knew that Léon hadn't liked her mother. In fact, she suspected that his feelings towards Celestine went beyond mere dislike. And in an odd way, it created an unexpected empathy between them because she understood those bitter emotions only too well; her whole life had been coloured by a deep resentment towards her mother.

She took another gulp at the brandy, shuddered deeply, then stared up at Léon.

'You'd better tell me the rest of it,' she said bluntly. 'There is more, isn't there?'

'Yes, there is,' he confirmed, his own mouth setting into a tight line. 'The lawyers will explain all the details, but I can give you the gist of it.'

Jessica began to feel confused again.

'Lawyers?' she echoed. 'But where do they come into it?'

His black gaze fixed on her coldly.

'My father died recently. The lawyers are dealing with

his will. And with the question of your inheritance.'

She gave a confused, baffled shake of her head. What on earth was he talking about now? Inheritance? What inheritance?

Léon growled a little impatiently under his breath.

'I keep forgetting that you know so little about this, that I've got to explain every damned thing.'

But quite suddenly she didn't want to hear any more. A wave of something very like claustrophobia was sweeping over her, she felt trapped, horribly breathless, she needed to get out into the fresh air.

'You don't *have* to explain anything,' she muttered unsteadily. 'I've heard quite enough for today, thank you.' She began to search a little frantically for her shoes. 'I want to go home now——' She couldn't find her shoes, but she didn't care, it wasn't important, she would go barefoot if necessary. All that mattered right now was getting out of here, for she couldn't stay in this room one second longer. She was quite desperate to get away from this cold, unfeeling man who had presented her with all those facts about her mother's life—and death—with such a disgusting lack of feeling, not caring in the least about the effect his blunt revelations would have on her. All right, so she couldn't pretend any deep grief at the news that her mother was dead. It had still come as a hell of a shock, though; she was shaking violently inside.

Before she could make a bolt for the door, Léon's strong hand shot out and his long fingers slid in a vicelike grip round her shoulder. A second later, she found herself pushed back on to the bed. Staring up at him, she caught her breath as she saw the dark emotions that flickered revealingly in the black depths of his eyes, and she gulped hard. Not as cool as she had thought. In fact, not cool at all; all that icy restraint was just a façade, underneath it surged a stormy violence that he was only just managing to keep under control. But why was she arousing all these strong feelings in him? She hadn't done anything—except to be born Celestine's daughter, she remembered a little bitterly. And it was pretty clear how he felt about Celestine.

'You're not going anywhere until you've been told everything you need to know,' he informed her curtly.

'That's what you think!' she retorted, with a brief upsurge of her old spirit. 'Who the hell are you to tell me what I can or can't do?'

'I'm your stepbrother,' he reminded her tersely, and for a moment that knocked all the fight out of her, forcing her to remember a lot of things that she would much sooner have forgotten. But then the need to get away from him rushed over her again. She had always been like that when something happened that deeply upset or hurt her. She wanted to bolt straight off to a quiet corner where she could sit and work it all out inside her head, find a way of coming to terms with it before she had to face the world again.

With fresh determination, she tried to struggle up, but his hand kept her relentlessly pinned to the bed. His black eyes were blazing down into her own, and a light flare of colour stained his cheekbones, making the deep scar stand out even more vividly.

'Stop being so childish,' he ordered angrily. 'You can't run away from this, Jessica, so just sit and listen while I explain——'

'I don't want to hear any more of your explanations,' she flung back at him in a voice that was openly shaking now. 'My God, don't you think you've told me more than enough for one day? Short of tying me to this bed, there's no way you're going to keep me here one minute longer, so let go of me you bullying——bullying *bastard*!'

For an instant, his eyes blazed as revealingly as her

own. All his muscles tensed, but then they relaxed a fraction again as he won the battle to hang on to his own self-control. Perhaps he had heard the note of near-hysteria in her voice, and had realised that she had no control over what she was saying any more, that she was just floundering in a quagmire of raw emotion.

'Get a grip on yourself, Jessica,' he advised much more steadily. 'This isn't getting us anywhere.'

But she couldn't get back her own self-control so easily, and a small part of her furiously resented the fact that he could keep his own temper on such a tight rein. She wanted to throttle him, see his face as darkly flushed as her own, his eyes glistening with a whole host of wayward responses as her hands went round his throat and squeezed and squeezed——

Shaken rigid by the shattering force of her own emotions, Jessica shuddered deeply, and desperately tried to get some kind of control over her rioting nervous system, to fight off the waves of pure rage that were pouring over her. She vaguely realised that it was shock that was making her react like this; the blinding discovery that her mother had remarried, casually ignoring the fact that she had a child by her first husband, cutting them both out of her life as if they had never existed. And now she was dead, she would never know how much Jessica had hated her for her callousness, her lack of love and concern.

The rage couldn't last for long at such an intense pitch. It slowly started to recede, and with an immense effort she forced all the pain and resentment back deep inside her, locking it safely away so that it couldn't hurt her any more. She lay on the bed, breathing quickly and irregularly for a couple of minutes, then her thundering pulse rate at last started to steady, and she began to feel ashamed of her hysterical outburst.

'It's all right, you can let go of me now,' she muttered in a low voice, not looking at him. 'I'm OK—and I'm not going to run away.'

He instantly released her, and she glanced down and saw the deep red marks of his fingers on her skin, marks which she knew would later darken to bruises.

'Brute,' she accused hoarsely under her breath, and she lifted her bowed head and stared up at him with heavy dislike. From the moment she had first seen him, she had instinctively known that there could never be any gentle emotions between them. They sparked something off in each other, were curiously aware of each other's presence. At first, she had been a little afraid that this uncomfortable awareness might all too easily turn into something else, something highly volatile and hard to handle. It was an enormous relief to find that it was only mutual dislike that was radiating from both of them. It would be far easier to cope with than those other, much more complicated emotions which she no longer trusted and had no intention of getting involved with ever again.

Léon prowled away, finally slumping down into a chair on the far side of the room. Jessica noted that he suddenly looked very tired, but she didn't feel the slightest twinge of sympathy for him.

'You were talking earlier about my inheritance,' she reminded him bluntly. 'Perhaps you'd better explain exactly what you meant.'

One black eyebrow lifted cynically. 'I thought you might be interested in hearing more about that.'

Jessica bit back a furious retort, and waited tensely.

'To put it very simply,' Léon went on, 'my father left you a half-share in the Château de Sévignac, our family home.'

She blinked hard. 'He—*what*?'

'Since your hearing isn't defective, I assume that you

heard me perfectly well the first time.'

Ignoring his unpleasant remark, Jessica continued to stare at him in disbelief.

'But—why on earth would he do a thing like that?'

'Because your mother persuaded him to, of course,' Léon answered in a hard voice.

'My mother——?'

'Don't try and fool yourself that she did it out of sentiment,' he warned her. 'It wasn't some kind of penance to make up for all the years she'd neglected you. Celestine didn't have a maternal bone in her body. I don't think she gave you—or your father—another thought after she'd walked out on you. She did it purely to get back at *me*. She probably found it very amusing that she'd managed to take a large portion of my inheritance away from me. We disliked each other intensely, as you've probably already realised.'

Jessica was still staggered by this latest revelation.

'But why did your father ever agree to such a thing?' she said slowly at last. 'Weren't you his eldest son——?'

'His only son,' cut in Léon. 'But that counted for nothing, not after his marriage to Celestine. She always came first. She was a cheat and a liar, but he loved her quite obsessively. While she was alive, he would do absolutely anything she asked. After she died, he went totally to pieces, he was like a walking zombie. In the end, his heart simply gave out. At least, that was the medical verdict. The simple fact was, he couldn't live without her.'

'Just like *my* father,' whispered Jessica a little numbly, suddenly forgetting everything else for the moment.

Léon looked up sharply. 'What are you talking about? Your father died in a car accident.'

'That was the official verdict,' she agreed with some bitterness. 'But there were so many rumours—I wasn't old enough to understand them at the time, but later on I remembered them, knew what people had been saying. You see, his car veered off a dead straight road and smashed into a wall. But they couldn't find any reason *why* his car swerved so violently. They checked the wreckage and couldn't find any trace of mechanical failure, and an autopsy showed my father had been in good health, he hadn't had a heart attack or anything. He hadn't even been drinking.'

'He could have fallen asleep at the wheel,' suggested Léon after a moment's silence. 'It happens sometimes.'

'He could have, but he didn't,' Jessica answered bluntly. 'Oh, the inquest didn't actually call it suicide, they finally brought in a verdict of accidental death, but no one who knew my father believed it.' She paused, gazing into space, dredging up memories which she usually kept safely locked away. 'All I can remember about my father is that he was always so quiet, so withdrawn,' she said softly, almost to herself. 'He'd go for hours sometimes without saying a single word. Aunt Lettie said he hadn't been like that before the divorce, it was only after my mother walked out that he changed so completely.' Her eyes darkened. 'How could my mother have had that kind of an effect on a man?' she said a little wonderingly. 'What kind of woman *was* she?'

Léon's face altered slightly, hardening around his mouth and eyes.

'Look in the mirror,' he said harshly. 'You'll find part of the answer there.'

Her clouded gaze rested on him in bewilderment. 'I don't know what you mean——'

He swung himself smoothly out of the chair, gripped her arm and hauled her to her feet. Before she could manage an outraged protest, he had pushed her over to stand in front of the full-length mirror on the other side of the bedroom.

'I could hardly believe it when I first saw you,' he told her tersely. 'It was almost like looking at Celestine all over again. The same dark hair and pale skin, even the same lush body. I wonder if you're like her in other ways as well?'

Jessica didn't really hear his last remark, she was still staring at her reflection in disbelief. She had had no idea that she looked like her mother; the only photo she had of Celestine was a blurred black and white snapshot she had found tucked away at the back of a drawer after Aunt Lettie had died. She knew her father had destroyed all the other photos after the divorce; this one must have somehow been overlooked. It had been too crumpled and faded, though, to give more than a vague impression of a tall, dark-haired woman, so Léon's words had come as a total shock.

And he had called her body 'lush'! Even Steven had never said such a thing to her.

With a small shiver, she closed her mind to all thoughts of Steven. Although in one way she was grateful to him, because he had taught her a useful lesson. It was dangerous to love someone, because it hurt too much when they weren't there any more. And Jessica had already lost too many people in her life. Both of her parents, Aunt Lettie, then finally Steven—each loss had seemed to hurt a little more than the last, and she couldn't face it happening again. After Steven had gone, she had reached a firm decision and stuck to it. She would have friends, but not lovers. A little loneliness was better than all that pain.

'*Are* you like your mother, Jessica?'

Léon's voice in her ear brought her sharply back to the present. With a small shock, she realised that his fingers were tracing their way slowly, almost idly, up her bare arm, leaving a trail of tiny goose-pimples in their wake as her body reacted with unexpected agitation to his touch.

She wrenched herself free of him, then moved quickly away.

'What the hell do you think you're doing?' she demanded angrily.

'I thought there might be more ways than one of persuading you to do the decent thing,' he answered, giving her an assessing and yet somehow disturbingly intimate smile.

'Exactly what do you mean by that?'

He quite deliberately misunderstood her. 'How did I mean to persuade you? I'd have thought that was fairly obvious——'

He took a couple of steps forward, and Jessica felt all her nerves twitch in alarm.

'Don't—don't you dare come any closer!'

To her utter relief, he stayed where he was, looking at her now with mocking amusement. Her heart was still thumping away so hard and loud that she was certain he must be able to hear its frantic beat echoing round the room. It dawned on her, a little too late, that this clever and calculating stepbrother of hers could be a very dangerous man to deal with. Yet she also had the impression that he wasn't quite as in control of his own deep-buried emotions as he would have liked to have been. Every now and then a small tongue of flame broke through that cool outer façade, a warning of the anger that burned fiercely far below the surface.

And she knew now why he was so angry. Her mother had managed to cheat him of part of his inheritance— and she had the uneasy feeling that he had no intention of accepting the situation, that he was coldly determined to do something about it.

'You said I should do the decent thing,' she reminded him stiffly. 'What do you consider the "decent thing" to be?'

'I would have thought that was perfectly obvious,' replied Léon, staring directly at her with those hard, black eyes. 'Since you've no moral right to any part of my father's estate, I expect you to renounce your claim, to tell the lawyers you don't want any part of it.'

The sheer arrogance of the man astounded her. How dared he stand there and tell her that she had no right to something that was legally hers? Especially after being so totally unfeeling and unpleasant! Just look at the way he had told her about her mother's death. He had just dumped it straight on her, he hadn't even tried to break it to her gently. The faint echo of the shock waves was still rattling round her nervous system. And now he was calmly informing her that he expected her to give up this inheritance which she had only just heard about; he didn't even want to give her a chance to find out anything more about it. If medals were ever handed out for pure insensitivity, this man could go to the front of the line and collect his straight away.

Her straight, dark brows drew together in a warning line as she glowered at him. He was about to find out it wasn't going to be easy to walk all over *her*.

'If I'm entitled to this inheritance, then I intend to claim it. Every single penny of it.'

Léon's eyes openly registered his total disgust. 'You *are* like your mother. I suppose I shouldn't really have expected anything else.' He strode towards the door, then paused briefly. 'I've got to go out,' he told her curtly. 'I'd prefer it if you weren't here by the time I get back. I'll pick you up at your apartment at eleven o'clock tomorrow morning.'

'What for?' asked Jessica warily.

His black gaze swept over her icily. 'To take you to see my father's lawyer, of course. I imagine you can't wait to find out exactly how much you're now worth.'

Then he left, slamming the door so viciously behind him that the whole room seemed to rattle. And Jessica drew in a shaky breath and sternly told herself that she wasn't frightened of Léon Castillon, of course she wasn't. It was just that she wished she didn't have to see him again in her entire life!

She got out of his apartment as quickly as she could. Half an hour later, she was back in her own tiny apartment, which seemed even more cramped than usual in comparison with Léon's luxuriously spacious rooms. Her legs still felt horribly weak, but that was hardly surprising after her bad experience last night, then being so bluntly told the truth about her mother.

The more she thought about the way Léon had broken it to her, the more indignant she got. No gentle sympathy, no warning of what was to come, just the straight facts and then a slug of brandy when she had looked as if she was about to keel over with shock. Léon Castillon might look ultra-civilised, but inside he was just a barbarian!

When she felt a bit more steady, she made her way down to the phone in the hallway and rang Maggie's number. When Maggie finally got to the phone and heard Jessica's voice, she gave a small squeal of concern and excitement.

'Jessica, are you all right? We rushed round when we heard about the fire, and we nearly died when we saw you being dragged out practically unconscious. Then you were carried off by that gorgeous man in that huge, flashy car—who was he? Where did he take you? Are you *really* OK?'

Maggie briefly ran out of breath, at last giving Jessica a chance to answer.

'I still feel a bit shaken up, but not too bad.'

'Better take it easy for the rest of the day,' advised Maggie. 'Anyway, it's no use going round to the theatre, it's total chaos everywhere. They're still trying to work out how much damage was done by the fire. Quite apart from the stuff that actually got burned, there's a lot of smoke damage. Dozens of the costumes are ruined, and of course everything's soaked in water. They reckon it could be weeks, perhaps even months, before the revue finally reopens. No one really knows for certain yet.'

'Do we get paid while the revue is closed down?' asked Jessica, with her usual talent for concentrating on practical matters.

'That's what just about everyone wants to know,' answered Maggie a little wryly. 'And so far no one's got a straight answer. I'll let you know as soon as I hear anything definite. Now we've got all that settled, let's get back to the interesting bits. Who *was* that tall, dark hunk who carried you off last night? Come on, Jess, let's have all the details—although I suppose you can leave out any truly erotic bits,' she conceded with some reluctance.

Jessica grinned. 'As a matter of fact, he took me straight back to his apartment. And I spent the night in his bed—silk covers, very sexy,' she crooned, grinning again as she heard Maggie's disbelieving gasp at the other end.

'I don't believe you——'

'It's the truth,' Jessica assured her solemnly. Then she relented a little. 'He didn't happen to be in the bed with me, though. I don't know where he spent the night. Sleeping on the sofa in the other room, I suppose.'

Maggie gave a disappointed sigh. 'What a waste! I wish it had been me he had rescued from the fire,' she said a little plaintively. 'I've always fancied being swept off by a tall, dark stranger. Are you going to see him again?'

'I haven't got a lot of choice,' grimaced Jessica. 'It turns out that he's my stepbrother.'

'I didn't know you had a stepbrother,' said Maggie in surprise.

'Nor did I, until last night.'

There was a thoughtful silence from the other end of the phone, then Maggie said, 'Well, at least he isn't a blood relation. That means there's nothing to stop the two of you——' She stopped tactfully at that point, and Jessica instantly jumped in.

'Don't start turning the whole thing into some romantic fantasy,' she warned. 'It's more likely to end in blood and bruises than hearts and flowers. You see, Léon's father has left me something in his will, and Léon—that's my stepbrother—isn't too thrilled by that.'

'Léon's father—he'd be your stepfather?' worked out Maggie.

Jessica blinked in surprise. 'Well—yes, he would,' she said rather slowly. She hadn't looked at it from that point of view before.

'It all sounds awfully complicated,' sighed Maggie. 'Why not call a truce, agree to share this inheritance with Léon, and then live together happily ever after? That's what I'd do. In fact, for a man like that, I'd give up the entire inheritance—providing I could have him in exchange, of course!'

'You wouldn't be saying that if you'd met him,' predicted Jessica darkly.

'I bet I would,' shot back Maggie promptly. 'Who needs women's lib and a career when there are men like that around?'

'I do,' said Jessica firmly. 'I happen to like being a dancer.'

'Sure, it's fun,' agreed Maggie. 'At least, it is for a while. But do you really want to spend the next ten or fifteen years hoofing your way round the world? I mean, it's not like ballet, is it? Our kind of dancing isn't exactly an art form, it doesn't need endless dedication and a lot of sacrifice.'

'We work hard,' argued Jessica defensively.

'Of course we work hard. And we have a good time. But that doesn't necessarily mean we want to go on doing it for ever. I certainly don't. Show me a man like your gorgeous stepbrother, and I'd be off after him like a shot.' Maggie paused. 'Look, Jessica, I've got to go, I've arranged to meet Sue for lunch. Want to join us?'

'No, I don't think so,' answered Jessica slowly. 'I'm not very hungry right now. I think I'll take a nap, then have something to eat later.'

'You're sure you're all right? I can come round later, if you like.'

'No, I'm fine. Just a bit tired.'

'I'll give you a ring then, as soon as I find out if we're being paid while the revue's closed down. 'Bye, Jess.'

Jessica trailed back to her apartment, then kicked off her shoes and stretched out on her narrow bed. Yet hard though she tried, she couldn't get to sleep. Her head seemed to be stuffed full of questions to which she didn't know the answers. What should she do about this inheritance which had suddenly fallen into her lap? She had told Léon that she intended to hang on to every penny of it, but was she really entitled to do that? Legally, she supposed she was. But morally? And what about Léon Castillon himself? And the rest of his family? She was related to them by marriage, they were the nearest thing she was ever going to get to a new set of relatives. Did she want to find out more about them? And about their home, the Château de Sévignac, where her mother had lived all those years as the Comtesse de Sévignac?

And if the answer to all those questions was no, what was the alternative? To go on dancing at the revue once it reopened, hoping that her contract would be renewed season after season? That conversation with Maggie had made her think seriously about several things which she had never considered more than fleetingly before. What was it Maggie had said about the kind of life they now led? 'It's fun—but that doesn't necessarily mean we want to go on doing it for ever'. Jessica sighed softly. She supposed Maggie was right. Most people thought they led a very exotic life-style, but in fact it was fairly limiting, with their social life severely restricted because of the hours they worked. Yet until now, she had been perfectly happy with the life she had carved out for herself.

Jessica sighed again, closed her aching eyes, and this time she slid instantly into a deep sleep.

By eleven o'clock the next morning, she was rather nervously waiting for the arrival of Léon Castillon. The clock on the mantelpiece struck eleven, and just a few seconds later she heard a car horn sound loudly and rather peremptorily in the street outside.

She pulled back the curtain, then her mouth dropped open slightly. On the night of the fire, she hadn't been in any fit state to notice what Léon's car was like. She couldn't help but notice it this morning, though. Huge and flashy—that was how Maggie had described it. And she had most definitely been right. It was also black and sleek and beautiful. Just the kind of car she would have expected Léon Castillon to have, thought Jessica with some scorn as she made her way down the stairs.

All the same, as they made their way through the streets of Paris, she had to admit grudgingly that it was rather nice to be cocooned in so much luxury. At least, it would have been if it hadn't been Léon Castillon at the wheel beside her!

So far, he hadn't said a single word to her. After several minutes, she glanced up at him with undisguised dislike.

'Is it your chauffeur's day off?' she enquired a little derisively.

'Why should you assume that I have a chauffeur?' he asked shortly, without even bothering to look at her.

Jessica shrugged. 'I wouldn't have thought that someone like you normally drove yourself.'

'Someone like me?' For a moment, he seemed genuinely surprised. Then the corners of his mouth lifted in a gently mocking smile. 'Ah, I see,' he went on softly. 'Someone wealthy and titled. Is that what you mean?'

'Of course that's what I mean,' she replied bluntly.

'And naturally I must also have a butler, a valet, a clutch of maids, a couple of cordon bleu cooks, and a whole gaggle of gardeners?'

'Now you're making fun of me,' Jessica said, a little sulkily.

'Only because you're being remarkably stupid,' he answered calmly. And there wasn't time for her to make an indignant reply, because at that moment the car drew smoothly to a halt in front of a tall, modern building.

Minutes later, Jessica was being shown into one of the inner offices. A rather dapper, silver-haired man was sitting behind a leather-topped desk, and he immediately got to his feet as Léon and Jessica walked in.

'Please take a seat,' he said. 'How are you, Léon? And this must be Mademoiselle Bryant.'

'Jessica, this is Henri Meyer, my father's lawyer,' Léon

said in a formal tone of voice.

Jessica greeted Monsieur Meyer in excellent French. Her command of the language had improved by leaps and bounds during the past few months, she was virtually fluent now and could follow any conversation with ease.

Henri Meyer began to flick through some papers on his desk, but Jessica could feel his gaze sliding briefly over her a couple of times. No doubt he was pretty curious about her, she thought to herself wryly. In fact, the entire Castillon family must be wondering exactly what she was like. Assuming, of course, that Léon *had* a family. He certainly hadn't mentioned them so far, but then, there hadn't been much opportunity yet for an ordinary, civilised conversation.

'I hope you are enjoying your stay in Paris, Mademoiselle Bryant?' Henri Meyer murmured courteously, breaking into her wandering thoughts.

Jessica was just about to reply equally politely when Léon cut in.

'Never mind the pleasantries, Henri. Let's get straight to the business in hand. I'm sure that all Mademoiselle Bryant is interested in is hearing how much she is worth.'

Henri instantly looked shocked, but he didn't argue with Léon. Instead, he rather unhappily reached for the top document in the neat pile in front of him.

'André Castillon's will is fairly straightforward,' he began.

'André Castillon?' cut in Jessica questioningly.

'Léon's father—your stepfather,' Henri explained.

'Oh,' she said, a little awkwardly. She still couldn't quite get used to the idea that she had had a stepfather all those years, and she felt a small twinge of regret that she had never had the chance to meet him. She had the feeling that she would rather have liked him.

'As I said, his will is quite straightforward, at least

where it concerns you,' Henri Meyer told her. 'It states
that you are to inherit a half-share in the Château de
Sévignac, and you also have the right to stay there at any
time, and for as long as you wish. As well as this, you are
to have a small annual income. It was André's wish that,
for your mother's sake, you were to be well provided for.'

Léon gave a brief snort which sounded like a cross
between contempt and disgust, but Jessica ignored him.

'I didn't know about the annual income,' she said, with
a frown. 'How much is it?'

When Henri Meyer told her, she felt her violet eyes
open wide with stunned disbelief. They regarded that as
small? Just how wealthy were these Castillons?

'Are you sure?' she croaked.

'Not enough for you?' enquired Léon caustically.

Jessica didn't even hear him, she was still staggered by
this latest revelation.

'Do you think you can manage on such a sum?' asked
Henri Meyer a little anxiously. 'If not, perhaps I could try
and persuade the family to be a little more generous——'

'She doesn't get a cent more than she's legally entitled
to,' Léon cut in tautly. 'Try and raise her allowance, and
I'll personally fire you, Henri.'

'There's no need for that,' Jessica stated furiously as
Henri went slightly pale. 'I can manage perfectly well on
that amount.'

And so she could. In fact, she could probably live very
comfortably for two or three years on what they proposed
to give her every year. And that was without counting her
salary from the revue.

'I have the first cheque for you here,' went on Henri. 'If
you would just like to sign this receipt, Mademoiselle
Bryant?'

A little shakily, she signed, then stared rather
awestruck at the cheque she now held in her hand.

'Are there any more papers for Mademoiselle Bryant to sign?' Léon asked abruptly. 'No? Then we'll leave now——'

'Wait a minute,' Jessica interrupted, as her confused mind at last began to clear. 'Where *is* this half a château I've inherited?'

'It's a few miles south of the Dordogne,' Henri Meyer told her. 'A very beautiful part of the country. I believe Léon is flying down there tomorrow. If you wish to see it, perhaps you could go with him?'

One look at Léon's face must have made Henri instantly regret his spur-of-the-moment suggestion.

'If Mademoiselle Bryant wishes to visit the château,' Léon said with soft venom, 'I suggest she makes her own travelling arrangements.'

It was odd, but until that moment she hadn't really thought of visiting the château. In fact, she hadn't quite been able to believe that half of this unseen château now belonged to her. But now she found herself thinking, why not? There was nothing to keep her here in Paris at the moment. It would be some time before the revue opened again after that disastrous fire. And quite suddenly, she was filled with a strong urge to see this château where her mother had lived for so many years; an irresistible curiosity was starting to surge up from somewhere deep inside her. It was as if there was a great gap in her past which she had unexpectedly been given the chance to fill.

She turned and looked at Léon with new determination gleaming in her violet eyes.

'I'll get to that château somehow,' she told him calmly. 'I'll take the train, the bus, hitch-hike, even walk if I have to. But one day you're going to open the door and find me standing on your doorstep. Why not save both of us a lot of trouble and just take me with you tomorrow?'

Léon's black gaze rested on her icily.

'I suppose the sooner you get there, the sooner you'll leave again,' he growled eventually.

Jessica smiled at him sweetly. 'I might like it so much that I'll want to stay indefinitely. I am legally entitled to stay as long as I please, aren't I, Monsieur Meyer?'

'Yes, you are, Mademoiselle,' agreed Henri, with a nervous glance at Léon.

Léon muttered something extremely rude under his breath, then he turned and strode angrily out of the office, slamming the door behind him.

'I must apologise for my stepbrother,' Jessica told Henri Meyer charmingly. 'He seems to make a habit of closing doors rather noisily. Thank you so much for all your help. Good-day, Monsieur.'

And it wasn't until she was standing on the pavement outside the lawyer's office that she discovered her legs were shaking rather badly. She drew in a deep breath and tried to relax her tense shoulders. She was going to the Château de Sévignac. With Léon Castillon.

Jessica decided that it was probably the most insane decision she had ever made in her entire life.

CHAPTER THREE

WHEN Léon had said that he would be flying down to the château, Jessica hadn't realised that he intended going in his own plane. Or that he would personally be at the controls. She was still rather surprised that he had actually agreed to take her. Of course, it wouldn't have made much difference if he had refused, she would still have got there in the end. She supposed that was what had finally made him change his mind. He would only have been postponing the inevitable.

Jessica peered out of the window. It was early evening now; they hadn't left Paris until late in the afternoon because Léon had had some business affairs to attend to first. There was still more than enough light for her to see the countryside over which they were now flying, though. Long valleys dotted with patches of woodland and strips of green fields, isolated farms and villages, and the occasional glint of water as a river wound its way lazily between the rounded hills. It looked quiet and peaceful, touched with a faint golden glow as the sun began to slide towards the horizon.

Léon had already told her that they would be landing at a small private air-strip not very far from the château. It was just about the only piece of information he had imparted since the start of their journey, and there had been something about the closed expression on his face that definitely hadn't encouraged her to start asking any more questions.

She nervously closed her eyes as the small plane circled round, preparing to land, but it wasn't necessary: it touched down so smoothly that she hardly felt the tiny bump as the wheels made contact. Glancing around, she saw that a car was waiting at the far end of the air-strip, and once their luggage had been retrieved from the plane Léon nodded towards the car.

'This way,' he told her.

Jessica picked up her suitcase and shoulder-bag, then trudged after him.

'A gentleman would offer to carry my case,' she muttered darkly under her breath.

Unfortunately, Léon heard her. 'And a lady wouldn't invite herself where she so obviously wasn't wanted,' he pointed out coldly.

She made a mental note to remember that his hearing was uncomfortably acute, hitched her bag a little higher on to her aching shoulder, and stoically plodded on.

There was a swarthy, middle-aged man waiting by the car. As Léon approached, the man opened the rear door for him, then took Léon's own luggage and began to stash it into the boot.

'I knew you had a chauffeur tucked away somewhere,' Jessica told Léon a little smugly.

Léon looked distinctly annoyed. 'Gustave also happens to be the handyman and gardener,' he replied irritably. 'I told you, I don't keep a large staff.'

Her own case and bag were put in the boot by Gustave, who shot her a couple of curious glances from under his heavy brows. Jessica was just thinking that it wasn't very polite of him to be so openly inquisitive when it dawned on her that he probably knew exactly who she was, and that was why he was showing so much interest in her. Léon had no doubt phoned ahead to the château to let everyone know that the daughter of the late Comtesse de Sévignac was about to waltz in through the front door, ready to inspect her newly acquired inheritance. And if that was the case, she was probably going to be the centre of a lot of attention and whispered speculation for quite some time.

The prospect didn't particularly please her, but there wasn't anything she could do about it, so she scrambled into the back of the car and collapsed on to the seat beside Léon.

'Is it far to the château?' she asked.

'We'll be there in just a few minutes,' Léon answered briefly. Then he turned his head away and rather pointedly looked out of the window.

Jessica could take a hint; she shut up and stared out of her own window. The sun was setting now, colouring the sky with smudged streaks of amber and cerise. The trees and fields had taken on a slightly mysterious glow, and the air felt soft, smelt sweet, brushed warmly against her skin as it flowed through the half-open window.

The car purred along, moving swiftly through the narrow lanes. She felt pleasantly relaxed, even slightly sleepy. A patch of woodland had cut out the last rays of the sinking sun, but then the car swept round a sharp bend, the trees were suddenly left behind, and they had an uninterrupted view of the valley stretching out in front of them.

Jessica blinked, blinked again, then gave herself a small, hard pinch to make sure she hadn't fallen asleep and started to dream. The pinch hurt, she was definitely awake. And she felt herself begin to gape a little disbelievingly at the scene which lay ahead of her.

'The Château de Sévignac,' Léon said softly, watching her reaction with his black, unreadable eyes.

She wasn't sure what she had been expecting, but it definitely hadn't been this. During the little free time she had had to think about it, her head had been filled with vague pictures of the elegant châteaux of the Loire.

Another illusion shattered, she thought to herself wryly; then her gaze slid up again to the dark silhouette of the Château de Sévignac.

Its jumble of towers and turrets were etched sharply against the blaze of colour that now filled the sky as the sun began to set. The château was set on a high outcrop of rock, its dark bulk looking strong and impregnable, as if it would stand there until the end of time. One side of the rocky outcrop fell away in a sheer drop to a river far below, while on the other side it sloped away more gently. Around the foot of the outcrop were a couple of dozen small houses, their red-tiled roofs reflecting the last of the sunlight, gleaming so brightly that they looked freshly painted.

'That's the village of Sévignac,' Léon told her. 'At one time, the village and all the land around here belonged to the château.'

She was certain that he wished it still did. It would have suited him down to the ground to have been some kind of feudal overlord, to have been able to look out of the windows and know he was lord of all he surveyed.

But the château *was* magnificent, even she had to rather grudgingly admit that. It totally dominated the valley, seeming to cast its fierce, dark shadow over the gentle countryside in much the same way that the Comte de Sévignac, sitting beside her, had cast a slightly menacing shadow over her own life.

The car swept on smoothly along the road, climbing steadily now. They passed through the main street of the tiny village of Sévignac, past the quaint little houses with their window-boxes and tubs overflowing with flowers, then the village was left behind and the road was climbing even more steeply. Seconds later, the car swung through a gateway and into a large cobbled courtyard, and the high walls of the château rose steeply all around them.

Still a little stunned, Jessica got slowly out of the car; then she looked around her with just a touch of awe. She still couldn't quite believe what she was seeing. And what was even more fantastic, half of this magnificent château now belonged to her!

'Trying to assess what your inheritance is worth?' enquired Léon rather unpleasantly.

Jessica refused to let even Léon spoil this moment for her.

'It must be impossible to put a price on a place like this,' she said almost reverently.

Léon merely looked cynical. 'If you're anything like your mother, you'll no doubt try. Shall we go inside?'

Gustave seemed to have taken care of their luggage, so she followed Léon up the stone steps that led to the impressive front entrance. As they approached it, one of the double doors smoothly swung open and a middle-aged woman greeted them with a broad smile.

'Welcome home, Monsieur le Comte,' she said.

'This is Madame Clemenceau, the housekeeper,' Léon said briefly. 'Madame Clemenceau, this is Mademoiselle Jessica Bryant.'

The housekeeper's gaze flicked over Jessica with the same curiosity that Jessica had already seen in Gustave's eyes. She gave a silent sigh. Was she going to be able to go anywhere in Sévignac without people staring at her and comparing her with her mother?

Then she was following Léon into the château, and almost immediately she forgot everything else as she stared, slightly goggle-eyed, at the blatant luxury which surrounded her. She had been expecting a lot of antiques, but this stuff was all modern. Luxuriously thick carpets and rugs, exquisite paintings, shimmering chandeliers and silk wall-coverings, all the different colours and textures combining to give the interior of the château an exotic, almost sensual appeal.

'Do you approve of the décor?' asked Léon with some acerbity. 'You should do, since your mother was responsible for every inch of it. Soon after she married my father, she decided that she didn't like all the "old furniture" that was already here, so she persuaded my father to sell all the priceless antiques that he had collected over the years. Then she completely refurnished and redecorated the interior of the château.'

'I think she did a fantastic job,' Jessica replied instantly; then was a little astounded as she realised that she had instinctively leapt to her mother's defence.

To her relief, Léon didn't comment on it. Instead, he glanced at his watch.

'It's getting late. Do you want something to eat? I expect Madame Clemenceau has prepared supper.'

The thought of trying to eat while Léon sat opposite her, fixing her with that fierce gaze from his black eyes, did absolutely nothing for her appetite.

'Perhaps I could have something in my room?' she suggested hopefully. 'If it's not too much trouble? In fact, I'd rather like to go up to my room straight away,' she went on, suddenly needing to find a little oasis of quiet where she could sit down and try to sort out her slightly muddled thoughts. 'Can you show me where it is?'

'First of all, I think we should go and pay our respects to my grandmother, before she retires for the night,' announced Léon. 'Since I very much doubt if you're going to enjoy meeting her, it would probably be best to get it over with straight away.'

Jessica swallowed hard. 'Your grandmother?'

Léon's black eyebrows shot up. 'Is it so very

remarkable that I should have a grandmother?' he
enquired.

'No—of course not. But you've never mentioned—I
wasn't expecting—did you tell her I was coming?'
gabbled Jessica, trying to fight off a sudden attack of
nervousness at the thought of being confronted with
another Castillon at such short notice.

'Of course I told her,' he replied with a touch of
impatience. 'It would be rather difficult to keep your
presence here a secret.'

'She isn't going to like me, is she?' she predicted a little
dolefully.

'Since she couldn't stand your mother, she'll most
likely feel exactly the same way about you,' Léon agreed
bluntly. 'Of course, you don't *have* to meet her,' he went
on in a much smoother tone.

'I don't?' echoed Jessica hopefully.

'Not if you don't want to. I can arrange for you to
return to Paris straight away.'

Instantly, she glared at him. 'You're not getting rid of
me that easily! All right, wheel out this grandmother of
yours. She can't be *that* much of an ogre.'

Léon didn't say another word. Instead, he took her
lightly by the arm and guided her up a wide sweep of
stairs that led to the first floor.

Jessica found herself wishing that he would release her
from that light but oddly disturbing grip. His fingers
were only resting very gently on her arm, but she would
much rather he wasn't touching her at all. In fact, she
didn't even like it very much when he simply came near
her. Léon Castillon had a disturbingly powerful physical
presence, and it did uncomfortable things to her nervous
system, it seemed to make her feel peculiarly off balance.
It was a great relief when he finally stopped outside a
door on the first floor and let go of her.

He knocked briefly on the door, turned the handle, then gently pushed Jessica into the room ahead of him. Then he followed her in, standing just behind her, far too close for comfort. Rather hurriedly, she took a few steps further into the room so there was a safe distance between them.

And what a room it was! The furniture was no doubt antique, but it was also old and dark, and the colour of the curtains had long ago faded. And what about all those mournful portraits on the wall? Long-dead Castillons? thought Jessica, with a wry twitch of her lips. And the carpet was nothing to write home about either, it was mud-coloured and patterned with an uninspiring design of sludge-brown leaves. If the rest of the château had once looked like this, no wonder her mother had been determined to completely redecorate and refurnish it. Who would want to live with a lot of priceless antiques when the overall effect was so depressing?

Then a door opened on the far side of the room, and Jessica instinctively drew herself up to her full height as an elderly lady walked into the room.

She had to admit that Léon's grandmother was a pretty impressive figure. Tall, her back ramrod-straight despite her age, she had the same strong physical presence that was so marked in Léon. Her iron-grey hair was drawn back into a tight bun that emphasised her still striking cheekbones, and she was dressed in black from head to toe, black dress, black stockings, black shoes, and above her sombre outfit glittered her bright, all-seeing black eyes.

Swallowing audibly, Jessica realised where Léon got his own extraordinary looks from.

'*Grand'mère*, this is Jessica Bryant,' came Léon's voice from just behind her.

His grandmother allowed her haughty glance to rest

very briefly on Jessica, then she looked away again.

'I can see perfectly well who she is,' she answered in an icily clear voice. 'She is quite unmistakably Celestine's daughter. But I see absolutely no reason why she should be allowed to come here, to this house.'

Jessica began to bristle at the old woman's imperious tone. She wasn't nervous any longer, just starting to get extremely annoyed. Who did these Castillons think they were? She wasn't a piece of dirt they could trample under their aristocratic feet whenever it so suited them!

'I was under the impression that half of this château now belongs to me,' she stated tightly. 'And that gives me every right to be here.'

The old woman's gaze flicked back to her, dark and contemptuous. 'Legally, it might belong to you,' she said haughtily. 'Morally, it will never belong to you, no matter how long you insist on staying here. A showgirl!' she sniffed in disgust. 'How fitting that Celestine's daughter should turn out to be a showgirl.'

'I'm a dancer, not a showgirl,' retaliated Jessica furiously. 'There's quite a difference.'

'There seems very little difference to me,' his grandmother replied with an expressive sniff. 'I'm told that a dancer simply takes off slightly less clothes than a showgirl.'

That did it! Jessica's temper simply exploded.

'You are a very rude old woman!' she yelled at Léon's grandmother. 'You might come from a long line of *comtes* and *comtesses*, but it's fairly obvious that no one's ever bothered to teach you basic good manners. And at your age, I suppose it's too late for you to learn now!'

And with that, she turned and rushed out of the room, knowing that she had to get out of there before she gave in to the almost irresistible urge to chuck something at the hateful old hag.

The trouble was, she didn't know where to go after that. The château was a rabbit warren of corridors, narrow passages and winding stairways. In her first fit of temper, she just rushed around aimlessly, but by the time she at last began to run out of steam, she realised she was hopelessly lost. The light was fading fast, and the château suddenly seemed full of dark corners and gloomy shadows.

She slowed down a little, then finally stopped, breathing rather heavily. What on earth should she do? Try and find her way back to the main hall, she supposed.

Inside, she was still angry and strung-up, her eyes were over-bright and she couldn't seem to see properly: everything was slightly blurred. Swinging round, she didn't even notice the tall figure who had silently come up behind her, and she cannoned straight into his hard, warm body.

'That was a fairly spectacular exit,' remarked Léon, catching hold of her as she stumbled off balance. 'And to think I was worried that my grandmother might intimidate you!'

'She was extremely rude,' Jessica mumbled furiously.

'You weren't particularly polite yourself,' he reminded her.

She knew that, and now her temper was starting to burn itself out she felt a small flicker of shame at the way she had acted. All the same, she wasn't going to give in that easily.

'I'm not going to apologise,' she warned stiffly.

'No one's asking you to. At least, not yet,' Léon replied, his voice unexpectedly calm.

A little belatedly, Jessica realised that his arms were still lightly linked around her. She knew that she ought to try and break free, but somehow she couldn't quite

summon up enough energy. All of a sudden she felt tired
and oddly disorientated, there was a loud thumping in
her ears and all her pulses seemed to be thundering away
at top speed.

I'll be all right once he's moved away from me, she told
herself rather dizzily. I wonder why he won't let go of
me? I won't fall over, I'm capable of standing on my own
two feet.

Then it occurred to her that perhaps *she* was the one
who ought to be making some effort to put some distance
between them. But when she tried to wriggle free, he
wouldn't release his grip on her, his arms stayed linked
behind her back, holding her prisoner.

Jessica stared up at him, beginning to feel distinctly
perturbed. They were standing in a heavy patch of
shadow, and she could see little more than the pale blur of
his face and the dark glitter of his eyes.

'I think—I think I'd like to go to my room,' she said
rather nervously. 'I'm really very tired.'

'Mmm,' murmured Léon, almost absently. He seemed
to be in an unexpectedly thoughtful mood, she could
almost hear his brain ticking over. She wished she knew
what he was thinking right now; then she decided that
perhaps she didn't want to know, after all. She might well
find it not at all to her liking.

For a few more seconds, they remained standing very
close together. Then Léon finally released her, and
Jessica immediately and rather hurriedly backed away.

'Will you show me where my room is?' she gabbled.

He gave the very faintest of smiles, as if he knew
perfectly well that her knees were gently quivering.

'Of course I will,' he agreed smoothly, and Jessica let
out a silent sigh of relief.

A few minutes later, they were back on the first floor.
Léon led her towards a door at the far end of the main

corridor, then opened it.

'I think you'll be quite comfortable in here. Gustave has already brought up your luggage, and I'll ask Madame Clemenceau to bring you your supper on a tray.' He paused and gave her a rather strange smile. 'Goodnight, Jessica.'

'Goodnight,' she muttered, and was thoroughly relieved when he finally turned and walked away.

She went into the bedroom, found her suitcase and started to unpack, but her mind was totally preoccupied with other things. Why had Léon been in such an odd mood just now? He hadn't even been particularly angry with her for being so rude to his grandmother. It was all rather puzzling—and just a little disturbing.

Despite everything that had happened, she slept unexpectedly soundly that first night at the château. Although she had half expected to find herself haunted by the ghost of her mother, nothing of the sort happened, for which she was thoroughly thankful.

In the morning, she woke up to find the sun streaming in through the unshuttered windows. She padded over on bare feet and peered out, then gave a small gasp. Just beneath her window, the walls of the château gave way to a sheer drop, where the outcrop of rock fell away sharply to the river far below. Jessica blinked slightly dizzily, then let her gaze wander further afield, past the river, across green stretches of grass, to the low hills which bounded the valley, shimmering softly in the early morning light.

'Fantastic,' she murmured appreciatively. Then, eager to explore further, she slipped off her pyjamas and dived into the bathroom. Thank heavens, the plumbing was modern! Her mother must have had it completely overhauled when she had had the château redecorated.

Minutes later, she was dressed and hurrying downstairs. As she reached the main hall below, Madame Clemenceau came out of one of the doorways.

'Ah,' said the housekeeper, with a smile, 'would you like some breakfast? Please follow me, I will show you where to go.'

She led Jessica to a small room at the back of the château. French windows opened on to a small terrace, where a table was laid for breakfast.

Jessica noticed that someone had been there before her. 'Has Monsieur Castillon already had breakfast?' she asked.

'He is always up very early,' the housekeeper told her. 'Which would you prefer, Mademoiselle Bryant? Coffee and hot croissants, or an English breakfast?'

'Oh, coffee and croissants will be fine,' Jessica answered. Then without thinking, she added, 'Which did my mother prefer?'

She had no idea why she had asked that question, it had just seemed to pop out from absolutely nowhere. It wasn't as if she was really interested, she had long ago decided that there wasn't a single thing she wanted to know about her mother.

'The Comtesse always had an English breakfast,' Madame Clemenceau answered, after a moment's hesitation. 'Although she was half-French by birth, she was very English in many ways.'

'Did you like her?' asked Jessica.

And she had no idea where that question had come from either. She had certainly had no intention of asking Madame Clemenceau any such thing.

'It isn't my job to like or dislike my employers,' the housekeeper answered diplomatically. 'I'll fetch the coffee and croissants,' she went on. And with that, she left the room.

Half an hour later, Jessica sat back and gave a

contented sigh. Her stomach was pleasantly full, the sun was shining warmly on her face, and she felt unexpectedly relaxed. This visit to the Château de Sévignac wasn't turning out at all as she had expected; in fact, she was almost beginning to enjoy it. Of course, meeting Léon's grandmother had been pretty grim, and Léon himself was still definitely an unknown quantity in many respects, but the château had already enchanted her. She could hardly believe she was lucky enough to actually own half of it.

Then the door opened and Léon strolled in. Jessica gave a small frown. There was always something to spoil a perfectly good morning.

He helped himself to coffee, then settled himself into the chair opposite her.

'Any plans for today?' he asked casually.

'Not really,' she answered. 'Why?'

'I thought you might like to begin the day by apologising to my grandmother,' came his calm reply. 'You've had a chance to cool down now, you should be able to make a fairly graceful apology.'

Jessica instantly bristled. 'I think that she should be apologising to *me*. She's the one who started slinging all those insults around.'

Léon stirred his coffee slowly. 'My grandmother is a very blunt old lady who always says exactly what she thinks,' he said eventually. 'It's just something that you're going to have to get used to. In view of her age, most people defer to her in this matter.'

'You mean, they let her get away with it,' retorted Jessica. 'Well, she's not going to walk all over me! I'm sorry I was so rude, but it was her fault, she started it. I was perfectly prepared to be polite to her, but she never gave me a chance.'

A little tensely, she waited for him to respond with his

usual quick flash of temper, but to her surprise he simply finished his coffee and it soon became obvious he didn't intend to say anything more on the subject.

Her gaze flickered over him, and for the first time she noticed he was wearing jeans and an open-necked shirt.

'Why are you dressed like that?' she asked, changing the subject.

His black brows rose expressively. 'Do you expect me to wear dark business suits here at the château?'

'Well—no—I suppose not,' she muttered, feeling more than a little stupid.

'As a matter of fact, I'm going to visit my uncle this morning,' Léon went on.

'I didn't even know you had an uncle.'

'There's a great deal that you don't yet know about me,' he pointed out. As she flushed slightly, he went on, 'He runs the Sévignac vineyard.'

'Vineyard?' repeated Jessica. 'I don't remember seeing a vineyard yesterday.'

'It's situated in the next valley, where the soil is more suitable,' explained Léon.

'Can I come with you?'

Her impulsive request caused him to frown darkly. 'You only own a half-share of the château, your inheritance doesn't include any of the other family assets,' he reminded her a little curtly. 'Anyway, you probably wouldn't find it in the least interesting.'

'Yes, I would,' she assured him immediately. 'Please let me come.' She was certain he was going to refuse, but to her surprise he gave a rather resigned sigh, then briefly nodded.

'All right. But you'll have to change into something more suitable. Have you got some jeans? And some flat-heeled shoes?' Jessica nodded. 'Then go and get changed, I'll meet you in the courtyard in ten minutes.'

She tried to be as quick as she could, but the zip on her jeans stuck and it was nearly a quarter of an hour later before she hurtled out into the courtyard, puffing breathlessly. There was no sign of Léon, though, and a dark suspicion began to creep into her mind. Perhaps he had never had any intention of taking her with him. Sending her upstairs to change her clothes might have been just a ploy to get her out of the way while he left without her!

She waited a few more minutes, then was just about to stalk back into the château, blazingly angry, when a rather familiar clopping sound caught her attention. Turning round, she stared towards an archway in the far corner of the courtyard. Then her eyebrows shot up in pure disbelief as she saw Léon coming through the archway, leading two absolutely enormous horses.

As he led them towards her, she stood with hands on hips, glowering at him.

'What's wrong with the car?' she enquired sarcastically. 'Run out of petrol?'

'I thought it would be a pleasant morning for a ride,' he answered blandly. 'Of course, if you don't want to come——'

Oh no, he wasn't getting rid of her *that* easily, Jessica decided furiously. She marched up to one of the horses, but then her nerve nearly failed her. It was huge, towering over her, its awesome bulk looking as unscaleable as the north slope of the Eiger. How on earth was she ever going to get on its back?

'Haven't you got—er—anything smaller?' she asked, trying to keep her voice very casual, as if the thought of getting on this massive horse really wasn't scaring her half to death at all.

'Smaller horses are often more skittish,' Léon pointed

out calmly. 'Isabelle hasn't got a skittish thought in her head. She's so placid that you'll probably have to give her a poke in the ribs now and then to stop her falling asleep. Do you want a leg-up?'

What she needed, thought Jessica a little desperately, was a ladder. She couldn't see any other way she was going to get into that saddle.

'Put your foot in the stirrup,' instructed Léon, showing her how. 'That's right. Now grasp the reins, hold on to the front of the saddle, and up you go——'

And after a lot of very undignified scrambling around, she was suddenly sitting on the horse's back, and the ground looked a million miles away. Jessica blinked nervously. 'What if I fall off?' she asked rather shakily.

'You won't fall off,' Léon answered patiently, swinging himself up into his own saddle with easy expertise. 'You're a dancer, aren't you? And dancers are supposed to have an excellent sense of balance. Just sit there and enjoy the ride.'

He made a soft clicking sound to his own horse, a glossy black stallion, and as it moved off, Isabelle plodded along placidly in its wake. For the first few minutes, Jessica was too terrified to move, she just clung on like grim death and silently vowed never to ask Léon to take her anywhere again. But then she slowly got used to the horse's jolting gait, she began to feel fairly secure on Isabelle's broad back, and after a while she was surprised to find that she was almost enjoying it.

Léon glanced back at her. 'Want to try a trot?'

Her new-found confidence instantly wavered. 'No!' Then she grinned wryly. 'Ever heard the old saying about learning to walk before you run?'

Much to her surprise, Léon grinned back. 'All right, we'll stick to a walk for a while.'

The horses wound their way through the quiet lanes,

the sun beat down warmly, and Jessica grew steadily more relaxed. After about three-quarters of an hour, Léon drew his horse to a halt and Isabelle also immediately stopped.

'Do you want to rest for a few minutes?' he asked. 'If you're not used to riding, your legs are probably beginning to ache a bit.'

And as a matter of fact, they were. And not just her legs, she admitted to herself drily. It was a relief to slide down to the ground and stretch her slightly cramped muscles.

Léon left the two horses to graze, then sprawled out in the shade of a nearby tree.

'You'd have reached the vineyard much quicker if you hadn't let me tag along,' Jessica remarked a little apologetically, as she seated herself a safe distance away from him.

'There's no hurry,' Léon answered comfortably.

She crossed her legs, then sat and stared at him thoughtfully.

'Do you mind if I ask you something?'

'I doubt if I could stop you,' he answered with a touch of resignation. 'What do you want to know?'

'Well——' She hesitated for a moment, then blurted out, 'I wondered how you got that scar on your face.'

To her surprise, he didn't growl at her to mind her own business. Instead, he fingered the scar lightly, then gave a slightly rueful shrug of his shoulders.

'It happened when I was quite young. Like most boys, I thought I was a lot cleverer than I actually was, and I was convinced I could climb a steep rock-face that my father had warned me several times to stay away from. About half-way up, I lost my footing and fell off. I broke a leg, cracked a rib, and gashed my face open on a sharp chunk of stone as I fell.'

Jessica winced. 'You must have been in a lot of pain.'

'It was quite a while before I was totally mobile again,' he admitted. Then his eyes glinted with amusement. 'But it did have one advantage,' he went on. 'It saved me from a severe thrashing for being so disobedient.'

She was still a little astonished at his openness, the unexpectedly amiable tone of his voice. Her gaze narrowing slightly, she stared at him with a faint frown of suspicion.

'Why are you being so nice and reasonable today?' she asked with a mixture of curiosity and wariness.

Léon had just relaxed back and closed his eyes. Now he opened just one eye again, and looked at her thoughtfully.

'Am I usually so very unpleasant?'

'Well, up until now I wouldn't exactly have described you as warm and friendly,' she answered with blunt honesty.

His other eye flickered open; now his black gaze was resting on her unwaveringly.

'Is that why you're frightened of me?'

His unexpected question sent her reeling off balance. 'Frightened? Of *you*?'

'That's what I said,' he confirmed. 'Whenever I come near you, you back off. When I touch you, I can feel you shrinking away. What is it about me that scares you so much?'

Jessica was astounded. She hadn't expected him to be so perceptive. But it didn't matter, she could easily bluff her way out of this.

'What a load of rubbish!' she said scornfully. 'I'm not scared of you—or of anyone, come to that.'

'All right,' said Léon calmly, 'that's easy enough to prove. Touch me.'

She gulped. 'What?'

'I thought it was a simple enough instruction. Touch me.'

'But—why on earth should I want to do a thing like that?' she blustered.

'Because I've discovered that I don't like it when people are scared to come near me. Not even when it's you.'

'Oh, thanks very much!' she retorted.

'Come on,' he said persuasively. 'Just a little simple hand to hand contact. Call it a whim, if you like.'

Only it wasn't a whim, she knew that very well. It was a challenge. What was he up to now? She didn't trust this man a single inch, and she wished she knew exactly what was going on inside that dark head of his.

Léon sat up and held his hand towards her, palm upwards, and she stared down at it with a mixture of wariness and fascination, noting the long, slim fingers, the well marked palm, the strong wrist. An interesting hand—at least, it would be if it didn't belong to Léon Castillon. She had already decided that she wasn't going to let one single aspect of this man impress or interest her.

But it didn't look as if she was going to be able to get out of touching him. If she came up with some feeble excuse, he was going to assume that she really was scared of him. And she wasn't! At least, not in the way he was implying. She just didn't want any—well, any involvement of any kind, she told herself firmly. That had been the rule she had lived by for the last year, and so far it had suited her very well. Friendship, but nothing more. Only, in Léon's case, she wasn't sure that she wanted even that.

Whatever she wanted—or didn't want—though, one thing seemed depressingly certain. If she didn't want him to start getting suspicious, she was going to have to touch him. Not that it could possibly do any harm, of course, it would be just like a brief handshake.

With a small sigh of resignation, Jessica gave in to the inevitable. She briskly held out her own hand, then let her palm close over his. See? she silently murmured to herself, it was easy, it was——

It was starting to go wrong. She sensed it at once, but didn't immediately understand what was happening. It began with a faint tingling in her skin, nothing more than a featherlight reaction from the nerve-ends just below the surface. Then tiny pools of heat seemed to form where their palms actually touched, spreading until they began to join up with each other, and the warmth increased, became still hotter, until it almost seemed to melt her skin, welding her to the man sitting opposite her.

Deeply disturbed, she snatched her hand away. Then she gazed down at her palm in bewilderment, almost expecting to see the mark of his palm deeply imprinted on her own.

Léon moved a little closer. 'Interesting,' he murmured. 'I don't think that either of us expected that. What do you think would happen if we took this experiment a little further?'

Jessica didn't really hear him, she was still trying to work out what was going on. It wasn't until she glanced up and found him leaning over her, so close now that he was little more than a dark, blurred shadow which blotted out the sun, that she realised what he intended doing.

'No!' she said sharply.

'But I'm afraid that I really do want to—just out of curiosity——' Léon told her softly. The hand that had had such a disturbing effect when it had touched her own was curled round her shoulder now, stopping her from pulling away from him. And before she could turn her head away, his mouth had found and caught hers, his lips warm, his tongue invasive, and Jessica was so bemused by the sensations he was arousing that she forgot to struggle. Her head was starting to reel, while deep inside her there was a strange warmth which seemed to be building to a small fire. And she was certain he could feel the heat of that fire because he gave a small murmur of satisfaction, his kiss changed in intensity, became more probing, more forceful, and she was astonished to find her body growing curiously languid, almost as if inviting him to go still further.

And he did, one hand sliding up to cup her breast, lingering there contentedly, supporting the soft weight in the palm of his hand. Jessica could hardly believe that any of this was happening, but the pleasurable sensations chasing through her body, curling round her nerve-ends, were real enough. So was the warmth of his palm against the curve of her breast, moving gently now, setting up a slow, delicious friction that made her catch her breath softly in confused delight.

Then from nowhere, a thought surfaced and broke through all the relaxed pleasure. It was never like this with Steven——

And at the thought of Steven, reality returned with stark force. She jerked back, her body suddenly tense; then she rubbed her mouth with the back of her hand, almost as if trying to wipe away the memory of Léon's kiss. She wasn't ready for this sort of involvement again. Not now, perhaps not ever. And certainly not with Léon Castillon!

Léon made no attempt to stop her as she wriggled away from him, then hurriedly scrambled to her feet. Instead, he watched her thoughtfully, a light frown showing on his face.

'Are you worried because we're stepbrother and sister?' he asked quietly at last. 'There's no need to be, we're not related by blood in any way. That kiss was perfectly legal.'

Jessica stared down at him coldly.

'That was the very last thing on my mind,' she told him, utterly determined now to convince him once and for all that that kiss had meant absolutely nothing to her. 'The fact is, I—I just don't find you physically attractive.'

For an instant, a flash of incredulity showed in those glittering black eyes.

Arrogant bastard! she thought furiously. He just can't believe he isn't totally irresistible to any female between sixteen and sixty. And she conveniently blotted from her mind the memory of how she had first responded to his kiss.

After that, neither of them said another word. As they remounted their horses, still in total silence, Jessica told herself that she had really handled the situation quite well. With luck, she had made sure that Léon Castillon wouldn't want to repeat that particular little 'experiment' at any time in the future.

All the same, the day didn't seem quite as bright and untroubled as it had when they had first started out that morning.

CHAPTER FOUR

As the horses trotted on towards the Sévignac vineyard, Jessica kept her eyes carefully averted from the man riding ahead of her. She also stubbornly ignored the funny warm glow deep inside her, and to her relief it slowly faded, then finally disappeared altogether. And after a while she found herself thinking, not of the man who had caused that mysterious glow, but of Steven, who had caused not a glow but deep pain and humiliation.

Looking back, she was a little surprised to find that it was the humiliation she remembered more than Steven himself. She could conjure up a vague impression of brown hair, blue eyes and a lean body, but nothing else, not even that famous smile which he had used to such devastating effect.

They had met when they were both doing a summer season at a seaside resort on the south coast. She had been with a dance troupe that did a high-kicking routine during the first half of the show, and an energetic modern dance sequence to a top pop record during the second. Steven had been quite high on the bill. He had been hoping this would be his break, that someone from radio or TV would hear of him and come down to catch his act. He was quite something on stage, the audiences loved him. He had a good singing voice, was a first-class comedian, and even did a few magic tricks during his fast-moving act. That was when Jessica had really got to know him, because he had wanted a girl to help out with the tricks. He had asked her if she would be his temporary assistant, since her dance routines were over by the time his act came on.

She hadn't had to do much, just walk on stage with the props and look sexy in a tight-fitting costume, but she had thoroughly enjoyed it. And when Steven had asked her out a few nights later, she had immediately said yes.

Looking back, she realised she had been flattered that he had singled her out from all the other girls in the show. And Steven had been fun, full of charm and energy, and bursting with self-confidence.

That hadn't been his only attraction, though. He had also had a large family who lived only a few miles away, and he soon began taking her home with him whenever they had some free time. It wasn't until she began mixing with his noisy, friendly family that she realised how lonely she had been since Aunt Lettie had died. It wasn't too long before the thought of marrying Steven, of being made a permanent member of his boisterous family, was all she dreamed about. And she did love him, she was sure of it; they would be idyllically happy together.

The only thing they ever argued about was her refusal to sleep with him. Frightened though she was of losing him to someone who wouldn't hesitate to say yes, there was still something inside her that couldn't quite let go, let her take that huge leap into the unknown.

Then came the party that followed the last night of the summer season. Jessica wasn't particularly worried that the show had closed: she knew Steven had had several offers, and she was sure he would work something out that would include the two of them. Feeling secure and happy, she drank far more than usual that night, and didn't notice that Steven was emptying his own glass twice as fast as anyone else.

Later on, he drove her back to her lodgings, then cut

the engine and looked at her.

'I don't think I'm very sober,' he said apologetically. 'Mind if I come in and have some black coffee, then ring for a taxi? I don't think I should drive the rest of the way home in this state.'

'Better be quiet then,' she giggled. 'You know I'm not allowed visitors after ten—and it's definitely a lot later than that.'

They made their way quietly up to her room, and while she made some coffee on her tiny two-ring stove, Steven slumped on to the sofa.

When she handed him the coffee, he instantly pushed it to one side.

'I don't want the coffee,' he murmured. 'I want you. Really want you, Jess. It's making me physically ill not having you, don't you know that?'

As always, she started to feel guilty at not giving him the one thing he really wanted. Sensing her indecision, he caught hold of her and pulled her down beside him, and her head immediately started to reel a little. She began to wish she hadn't drunk all that wine. Then his hands seemed to be wandering all over her and it was funny, she was sure that she loved him, but she didn't really like it very much, and she wondered if there was something wrong with her, no one was still a virgin at her age— perhaps it was time to find out——

Realising that she wasn't resisting him as strongly as usual, Steven quickly and confidently lunged forward, pinning her to the sofa. And the whole thing rapidly turned into some kind of unreal nightmare after that, as far as Jessica was concerned. Stiff and awkward, all her muscles tense, every move he made seemed to hurt her, she could hardly believe that all this undignified groping was meant to bring some kind of pleasure. She desperately wanted him to stop, but knew that he wouldn't—probably couldn't. Then the wine began to churn in her stomach, she felt horribly sick, and in the end she just prayed that the whole thing wouldn't last too long.

It didn't. Steven had drunk much more than she had, and his self-control was non-existent. It wasn't long before he gave a final deep grunt of satisfaction, rolled away from her and instantly fell asleep.

Jessica stared blindly into the darkness. It'll be fine once we're married, she told herself doggedly. We'd both had too much to drink, that was all. It won't ever be like this again. Next time it'll be different, he'll be more careful and I'll enjoy it, I know I will.

Only there never was a next time. When she woke up in the morning, Steven had gone, and she never saw him again.

At first, she couldn't believe he had just walked out on her. But when she hadn't heard from him for a couple of days, she quietly began to ask around and found that no one knew where he was, they just knew he had gone. Someone said they had heard he had taken a job in a club up north, but it was only a rumour, and anyway, they couldn't remember which club it was.

Jessica knew that she could always ring his family and ask them, but somehow pride just wouldn't let her. With money running short now that the summer show was over, she took a temporary job as a waitress so she wouldn't have to move out of the area. She kept trying to convince herself that Steven would eventually come back looking for her.

Then one day she saw his older sister, Barbara, walking through the shopping precinct. On impulse, Jessica ran over to her. Once face to face with Barbara, though, she found she didn't know what to say. And from the slightly embarrassed look on the other girl's face, it was humiliatingly obvious that Barbara was only too aware of what had happened.

'You look awful,' Barbara said at last, in a very practical tone of voice. 'Come and have a cup of coffee.'

'My lunch hour's nearly over,' Jessica muttered awkwardly. 'I ought to be getting back.'

'After we've had a talk,' Barbara insisted firmly, and she steered Jessica towards a quiet corner of a nearby café.

'I always used to feel rather sorry for you,' Barbara went on, after they had sat down. 'You were obviously in love with Steven, and I knew this would happen eventually. I suppose I should have warned you, but I kept telling myself it was none of my business. And anyway, you probably wouldn't have listened to me. None of the others ever did.'

'Others?' echoed Jessica dully.

'You don't think you're the first, do you?' said Barbara bluntly. 'Look, Steven's my brother and in a lot of ways I'm very fond of him, but he's also a louse. Every time he gets a new job, he picks out the brightest, prettiest girl in the company and moves in on her. Then, when the show finally closes, he just walks away.'

'But he took me home to meet you—to meet all his family,' Jessica said in a low voice.

'He brings them all home,' Barbara told her. 'He reckons it softens them up, makes them think—well, the same thing that you thought,' she finished sympathetically. 'But no one will ever tie Steven down, he's deaf to the sound of wedding bells. He's ambitious and he likes a good time. Settling down doesn't figure in his plans for the future at all.'

But there was one other thing that had been preying on Jessica's mind, and quite suddenly she just couldn't keep it to herself any longer.

'We—we went to bed together,' she blurted out. 'I was awful. I thought——'

As her voice trailed miserably away, Barbara reached over and took hold of her hand.

'Listen, kid, you could have been the most fantastic lover in the world, and it still wouldn't have made him stay. And anyway, if I know my brother, he probably didn't even notice if you were good or not. He's pretty self-centred, all he ever really thinks about is what *he* wants, so if he was satisfied then that was probably enough for him.'

It should have helped, but somehow it didn't, and Barbara was shrewd enough to see it.

'Look, you've just got to face facts,' she said to Jessica, gazing at her steadily. 'The whole thing was one-sided right from the start. You fell in love, but all he really wanted was a bit of fun.'

'Why didn't he tell me that?' mumbled Jessica. 'Why couldn't he just have been honest?'

'Do you really want to know?' asked Barbara.

Jessica nodded.

'All right, but remember that you wanted me to tell you. It's because a girl who thinks she's in love will often do things that a girl won't, if she isn't. Once a man gets you to fall in love with him, all the advantages are on his side. You'd better remember that in the future.'

Jessica's eyes had gone very dark. 'Oh yes, I'll remember it,' she said softly but with great vehemence.

And she had. She didn't intend to lay herself open to that kind of hurt and humiliation ever again. No more one-sided affairs, in fact, no affairs at all. It was far safer that way.

Jessica opened her eyes, and for a couple of seconds she found it hard to remember where she was. Then her gaze focused on the straight-backed figure ahead of her riding the glossy black stallion, and she abruptly remembered everything; more than she wanted to, in fact, because she also found herself remembering how the kiss of this man had somehow affected her on a level that all of Steven's impassioned lovemaking had never even touched.

Be careful, she told herself silently. Léon Castillon doesn't like you, he deeply resents you for taking away part of his inheritance. Don't let him get to you, or you'll end up the loser—again.

At that moment, Léon reined his horse to a halt.

'There's the vineyard,' he said, pointing ahead of him.

The road had just breasted a low hill, and the valley that lay ahead of them was very different from the one they had left behind. There was no château, no village, no fields and woodland, just neat little squares patterned with geometrically straight rows of vines, and to their left a long, low house with a few chickens pottering around outside.

They prodded the horses into a lazy walk again, and as they drew nearer, Jessica could see the bunches of grapes on the nearest vines, the fruit just beginning to swell.

'They won't be harvested until the autumn,' Léon explained. He seemed to have recovered his temper now; his voice was a little cool, but quite calm. 'After the harvest, the vines have to be pruned, then there's a second pruning in March. During the summer, while the grapes are ripening, we bottle last year's wine. Then in the autumn, this year's grapes are picked and pressed, and the whole process begins all over again.'

'You make it all sound fairly simple,' Jessica remarked.

Léon raised one black brow. 'That's because I'm not a wine-grower,' he said drily. 'I merely look after the financial and marketing side of the business. My uncle would probably spend all day telling you how he actually produces the wine. He would explain that a great part of it depends on the instinct of the *vigneron*, the wine-grower, that there's a certain amount of mystique involved in producing a truly great wine.'

They were approaching the house now. It looked like an old farm, slightly ramshackle but very sturdy with its stone walls and tiled roof. As Léon slid easily from his own saddle, then helped Jessica to slither awkwardly down to the ground, a man strolled out from the house to meet them.

Jessica stared at him with open curiosity. He was very obviously a Castillon, as tall as Léon and nearly as dark, although his hair was flecked with silver streaks. There was something about his face that was softer, though, a kindly glint in his eyes which she had never yet seen in Léon's.

He was gazing back at her with equal curiosity, and a total lack of hostility, which Jessica found refreshing. Had she actually found a Castillon who was prepared to like her? She smiled at him a little shyly.

'You must be Celestine's daughter,' he said cheerfully. 'I'm Claude Castillon. I didn't know you were coming over with Léon this morning.'

'I didn't know either, until the last minute,' remarked Léon.

'Did you have a pleasant ride?'

'It was—very interesting,' Léon answered, with a slow

smile, and Jessica felt a faint flush of colour seep into her skin because she knew that he was referring to that kiss.

Claude shot his nephew a slightly exasperated glance. 'Léon, won't you give the child a chance to answer for herself?' Then he looked a little doubtful. 'Or does she not speak French?'

'She speaks excellent French,' Léon assured him. 'So be careful what you say in front of her, she'll understand every word.'

Claude looked at Jessica and grinned.

'Unless we somehow get rid of my nephew, we're never going to be able to have a decent conversation. Léon, why don't you go into the office and deal with the books? And I will take this young lady—Jessica, isn't it?—down to the cellars to taste my wine.'

Léon didn't seem too pleased about that arrangement, but there wasn't anything he could do about it, Claude had already put his hand on Jessica's shoulder and was leading her towards a nearby door. A flight of stone steps inside led them down into gloomy darkness. Then Claude flicked a small switch, and Jessica blinked as a weak electric light illuminated the low-ceilinged cellar that stretched ahead of them. Great black barrels were ranged along either wall, two long lines of them marching off into the shadowy distance, and Claude gave a small sigh of contentment as he ran his hand lovingly over the curve of the nearest barrel.

'Last year's wine was excellent, one of our best,' he said with deep satisfaction. 'But wait, I shall let you taste it for yourself.'

He disappeared into the depths of the cellar, then returned a few moments later carrying a small tray with two glasses on it, and a pipette. Then he carefully removed the bung on the nearest barrel, and dipped the pipette inside. Deftly, he transferred the wine from the pipette to the glass, then he held it out to Jessica, who very much hoped that she was going to like it. She had the feeling that Claude Castillon judged people solely by their reaction to his wine!

She sipped it, then grinned happily. It was delicious, fresh and delicately fruity, with just a faint undertone of dryness.

'Mm, I could drink gallons of this,' she said appreciatively.

'Then we would most likely have to carry you home,' Claude observed gravely. 'But I'm pleased that you like our wine.'

Jessica finished the glass, then regretfully refused another. 'I'd better not—not on an empty stomach.' She looked at Claude thoughtfully. 'Léon said earlier that he ran the business side of the vineyard. I wouldn't have thought that was a full-time job. Does he do anything else?'

Claude looked at her with some amusement, suddenly looking startlingly like Léon.

'He—er—dabbles in one or two other things.'

'What kind of things?' asked Jessica.

'Well, he has full charge of the family's finances and investments. Léon knows about money, while I'm afraid I'm very ignorant about business matters. But of course, even that's just a sideline.'

'Then what does he actually *do*?'

'What he enjoys doing most of all is buying up small companies that are about to go under, and putting them back on their feet again. Have you heard of Fenniman Plastics?'

'Didn't it hit the headlines a while back?' recalled Jessica with a small frown. 'It was about to go bankrupt, but then some whizzkid stepped in and virtually turned the company upside down. Now it's started to churn out the most amazing profits——' She paused, her eyes opening very wide. 'That was *Léon*?' she said disbelievingly.

'One of his more spectacular successes,' confirmed Claude. 'He's had a few small failures along the way, of course, but not many, and they were mainly at the very beginning. He's very interested in investments, as well. Have you seen his office at the château?'

Jessica shook her head a little dazedly.

'It's equipped with all the latest electronic gadgets. Information streams in from all the major stock exchanges as soon as they open. Léon says that the world of business is like a complicated board game. As long as you learn all the rules and are prepared to gamble every now and then, you can't help but make money.' Claude gave a small shrug of his shoulders. 'Léon understands money in the same way that I understand wine. It's a gift.' He was silent for a few moments, then he said unexpectedly, 'You really are extraordinarily like your mother.'

'That's what Léon said.' She hesitated, then added, 'Léon didn't like my mother, did he? He told me that when we first met, but I still don't really understand why. Oh, I know that he thinks she cheated him of part of his inheritance, but there's a lot more to it than that, isn't there?'

Claude gave a small sigh. 'I'm not sure that you really want to hear about it.'

'Look, my mother ran off and left me when I was three years old,' Jessica said bluntly. 'She was a stranger, I never knew her. You're not going to hurt me by telling me the truth about her.'

Claude still seemed reluctant to talk, but at last he leaned against the barrel behind him and looked at her.

'Léon was thirteen when your mother married my brother, André. It's a difficult age for a boy—not quite child, not quite man—and your mother deliberately went out of her way to make it even harder for him.'

'In what way?'

'It's difficult to explain,' Claude said, a little uncomfortably. 'As you said, you never knew Celestine, you didn't know what she was like. There were so many sides to her character, she could be charming, sophisticated, endearing, even childlike. Other times, she was—much less likeable.' Claude hesitated briefly, then went on in a quiet voice, 'Not long after she married André, she began to tease Léon—tease him sexually, I mean. Am I shocking you?' he asked, rather worriedly.

Jessica shook her head slowly. 'No. Please go on.'

'I'm sure she never intended to take her perverse games to the ultimate conclusion, it was the teasing she enjoyed, like a child playing rather cruel games with a kitten. But Léon didn't know how to handle it, he wasn't old enough or experienced enough. Yet he refused to tell his father what was happening. He knew that André was crazily in love with his new wife, and he stubbornly refused to do anything that would hurt his father. It was years before he even told me. And of course, he never forgave Celestine for all the torment and misery she put him through.'

'But why did she do it?' Jessica asked in a slightly horrified tone.

'I can only guess at that,' sighed Claude. 'There were a great many things I never really understood about Celestine. André only ever saw one side of her, the sweet and loving side. With the rest of us, she wasn't nearly as careful, and we all too often saw sides of her that weren't at all pleasant. I do know that she was desperately insecure. Looking back, I think what she really wanted was to cut André off from the rest of his family. That way, she could have him all to herself. And as far as Léon was concerned, she eventually succeeded. As soon as he was old enough, he left home, and he only rarely returned to the château after that. I'm sure that was her aim from the very beginning, to drive Léon away.'

Jessica's mouth twisted in disgust. 'What a cruel thing to want to do.'

'I suppose it was all part of her insecurity,' Claude said slowly. 'She wanted André's full attention every second of the day and night, and she didn't want anything—or anyone—to take that attention away from her. She saw Léon as a threat, and so she set out to get rid of him.'

'She must have been totally selfish!'

Claude nodded. 'Yes, I'm afraid that she was. It never seemed to occur to her that Léon had already lost his mother, that he might desperately need his father's affection. Celestine didn't seem to have any maternal feelings at all. But then,' he said with a sympathetic shrug, 'I suppose you already know that only too well.'

Yes, she did. But God, how it still sometimes hurt! With a tremendous effort, she forced back the pain and looked at Claude.

'But Léon was your brother's only son. Didn't André realise what was going on, see that his son needed help?'

'André was in love,' Claude said simply. 'He didn't see anything except Celestine. He adored her, he was besotted with her. There was really no reason for her to feel insecure, he would have done absolutely anything for her.'

'Like agreeing to leave me a half-share of the Château de Sévignac in his will,' said Jessica slowly.

'Yes,' agreed Claude, with a small frown. 'Léon was not pleased when he found out about that.'

'That's something of an understatement,' answered Jessica drily. Then she gave a small sigh. 'What a huge mess it all is.'

Claude looked at her thoughtfully.

'What will you do with your share of the château?'

'I've no idea,' she confessed. 'I only found out about it a couple of days ago, so I've not really had much chance to think about it.'

'Take your time, don't rush into any decisions,' he advised. 'You've just stepped into a whole new world. Give yourself a chance to get to know it better before you finally decide what to do.' He glanced at his watch. 'It's nearly lunch time. Are you hungry?'

Surprisingly, she was.

'Then let's go and eat,' he said, and he led her back up into the sunshine.

Lunch turned out to be a relaxed and pleasant meal, mainly because of Léon's lazy good humour. Jessica had never seen him in this sort of mood before, and she began to realise that he could be extremely charming, if he so chose. In fact, if it hadn't been for everything that had gone before, she would have found it remarkably easy to have been rather dazzled by all that effortless charm.

And as they finally took their leave of Claude and began to make their way back to the château, the two horses walking slowly in the heat of the late afternoon sun, she kept shooting furtive glances in Léon's direction whenever she thought he was looking the other way. A small part of her was trying to equate this self-possessed man with the boy who had been confused and hurt by her mother's perverse teasing. She even found herself feeling a sharp twinge of pity for him. It must have been hard enough to readjust when his father remarried, without having to endure a lot of sexual taunts from his new stepmother.

At that precise moment, Léon turned and looked at her.

'Have I just grown two heads?' he enquired a little caustically.

Jessica instantly flushed. 'Not that I've noticed,' she mumbled.

'Then why are you suddenly finding me so fascinating?' His voice changed to a low, deliberate purr. 'Would you like to stop for a while, so you can study me in more detail?'

She didn't answer, and kept her gaze glued to the ground after that. Idiot! she told herself furiously. Just because he had been inexperienced and unsure of himself at thirteen, that didn't mean he hadn't long since made up for it. And she had better make sure she remembered that in future, or she could easily find herself in a whole lot of trouble.

CHAPTER FIVE

JESSICA spent the next couple of days trying to keep out of everyone's way, which wasn't too difficult considering the size of the château and its grounds. She only saw Léon at mealtimes and occasionally in the evening, and to her relief she discovered that his grandmother rarely left her own suite of rooms. There were enough problems to cope with at the moment, without having to worry about having endless arguments with the haughty and outspoken old woman.

She spent quite a lot of time exploring the interior of the château. After all, half of it was hers, she told herself firmly, so she had a perfect right to go wherever she pleased. It was impossible to see all of it, though: a couple of wings were closed up completely, and several of the rooms in the main wing had locked doors. She asked Madame Clemenceau if she knew where the keys were, but the housekeeper looked a little awkward, then shook her head and mumbled something about those rooms not being used any more. Jessica decided not to make an issue of it, she wasn't *that* interested in seeing inside them. Instead, she found a secluded corner in the rather overgrown garden at the back of the château, then settled down to do some serious sunbathing.

She had to be careful when she sunbathed, all the dancers in the revue did. It didn't go down too well if you turned up with beautifully tanned arms and legs, but a lily-white body and strap marks which showed up all too clearly once the skimpy costumes were put on.

Since she hadn't bothered to pack a bikini, not thinking she would be needing it, she instead stripped off to her white cotton bra and pants. They were as decent as any bikini, but brief enough to let her tan every inch of her body which would show when she was back on stage.

It was marvellously peaceful in the garden. Nothing moved except the clouds of butterflies which drifted from bush to bush, the busy insects, and the swifts and swallows darting endlessly overhead. Jessica gave a small sigh of pure contentment and closed her eyes. If the girls from the revue could see her now, they would turn pea-green with envy. This place was just perfect—at least, it would be if there weren't too many Castillons around for comfort!

Suddenly, her skin didn't feel quite so warm. Oh damn, she thought irritably, was it clouding up? But there hadn't been a cloud in the sky just a few minutes ago——

She half opened one eye and squinted up, then both eyes shot wide open and she sat up indignantly. The 'cloud' was Léon Castillon, who was standing over her and completely blotting out the sun.

'Enjoying the view?' she enquired acidly. 'Why not pull up a chair so you can stare at me in comfort?'

'There's no need for that,' he answered with a lazy smile. 'I'm already perfectly familiar with the rather delectable sight of your body.'

The heat that was rushing over her skin now didn't have anything to do with the warmth of the afternoon.

'What have you been doing?' she accused hotly. 'Staring at me from behind a bush?'

He merely looked amused. 'There was no need for that. Do you see that window?' He pointed to a nearby window, the only one close by that directly overlooked the garden. 'That happens to be the window of my office,' he told her. 'And I must admit the view has been most interesting for the past hour.'

Feeling at a distinct disadvantage sitting there in just her bra and pants, Jessica wriggled into her dress and hurriedly did up the tiny buttons at the front. Fully dressed again, she turned on him with renewed hostility.

'I suppose it never occurred to you to let me know you were there?' she demanded angrily.

'Of course it occurred to me,' Léon replied, sounding infuriatingly relaxed. 'But I managed to overcome the impulse fairly easily.' Then, seeing her fast-rising colour, he added, 'Why are you making such a drama out of absolutely nothing? You go on stage wearing costumes that are little more than a few sequins sewn on a wisp of chiffon, you probably sunbathe on the beach in a very brief bikini, but for some reason you're getting unreasonably worked up over the fact that I've seen you in that very modest underwear.'

Jessica opened her mouth, ready to rage at him again, but then abruptly shut it. He was right. It really galled her to admit it, but for some reason she was getting totally worked up over nothing. With a huge effort, she choked back a bad-tempered retort and instead sat there in slightly sulky silence.

'That's better,' he said approvingly. 'And now that you're in a more reasonable frame of mind, I'll tell you why I'm here.'

'To get a closer look, I expect,' she couldn't resist muttering under her breath.

Léon's eyes glittered with a first hint of impatience. 'You've got a very nice body, but so have hundreds— thousands—of other girls. Yours certainly isn't so exceptional that I'm going to rush out because I can't wait to see it at close quarters.'

Jessica didn't know if she felt humiliated, insulted or blazingly angry. And while she was still trying to sort out her hopelessly mixed-up reactions, Léon calmly held up his hand.

'I can't remember how we got involved in this conversation, but I suggest we drop the subject right now. It's beginning to get rather boring.'

'If I bore you that much, why are you still here?' she challenged.

'I'm beginning to wonder that myself,' came back his slightly exasperated response. 'The fact is, I originally came out to ask you if you wanted to come with me to see the *caverne* in Sévignac.'

'What's that?' she asked, her curiosity stirring despite all her efforts to suppress it.

'No one's told you about it?' he asked in some surprise.

She shook her head. 'I haven't spoken to anyone much these past couple of days,' she confessed.

'Haven't you been down to the village of Sévignac?'

As a matter of fact, she had. But everyone had stared at her with such frank interest that she had scuttled straight back to the château. It was pretty obvious that Celestine Castillon had made quite an impression on the people of Sévignac, and now they couldn't wait to see what her daughter was like.

'Do you want to come to the cavern or not?' Léon asked again.

Jessica gave a small shrug and got to her feet. 'I've nothing better to do, so I suppose I might as well come with you,' she conceded.

'Such a gracious acceptance of my invitation,' he mocked gently. Then, before she could dredge up a scathing reply, he had moved off, walking at such a fast pace that it took her a while to catch up with him.

He led her along a path that wound its way down through the garden, then dropped even more steeply as it circled round to the foot of the high, rocky outcrop on which the Château de Sévignac stood. Jessica was puffing slightly by the time the path finally started to level out, which reminded her that she had missed out on her exercise periods since coming to the château. Whether she was dancing or not, she liked to do a rigorous half-hour daily work-out to keep her muscles supple and trim.

The trees ahead of them began to thin a little, and she caught a glimpse of water glittering in the sunlight. She realised that it was the river she could see from her bedroom window, and she briefly glanced back behind her, catching her breath a little as she saw the château towering high above them on its pinnacle of rock. She still couldn't get used to the idea that half of it now belonged to her, and she wasn't sure that she ever would.

A little further on, the path ran right down to the river's edge, and Jessica saw a small jetty, with half a dozen rowing-boats moored to poles set along one edge.

'Are we going in one of those?' she asked, staring at the boats a little suspiciously.

'That's the general idea,' agreed Léon.

He climbed easily into the nearest boat, untied it from the pole, then glanced up at her questioningly. 'Are you getting in?'

'I don't like boats,' she warned him. 'I get seasick.'

Léon's black gaze registered pure disbelief. 'Jessica, this is a small river, not the Atlantic! And we won't be in the boat for more than a few minutes. I promise you will not get seasick.'

'Don't bank on it,' she said pessimistically, but she

scrambled awkwardly into the boat all the same, sitting gingerly on the wooden plank at the far end, which served as a seat.

Léon picked up the oars and expertly began to row, sending the boat shooting away from the jetty. She realised they were heading straight towards the high, sheer cliff-face, and she stared a little nervously at Léon and wondered if he knew what he was doing. He must do, she assured herself, he had lived here most of his life, he wasn't going to row them straight into that wall of solid rock.

Only he gave every impression of intending to do just that. The cliff loomed nearer, the small boat zipped along without slackening speed, and Jessica was just nervously wondering if there would be time to jump overboard before they actually smashed into the rock when she saw a dark, narrow fissure directly ahead of them. A minute later, Léon slackened pace a little and the boat drifted through the fissure, which widened considerably as soon as they were through the entrance. Jessica blinked, it was hard to see anything very clearly after the brightness outside. There didn't seem to be anything ahead of them, though, except thick, black shadows.

Just then, she noticed a small wooden box set in the wall. Léon reached towards the box, opened it, then pulled down the switch inside. A blaze of electric lights instantly shone out, and Jessica sat there and gaped in sheer amazement at the sight which now confronted her.

Ahead of them, brightly illuminated by a string of electric lights set high overhead, was a huge cavern which stretched right back into the cliff. Fantastic rock formations loomed all around them, and majestic stalactites hung suspended from the roof, like giant icicles, their reflections dancing in the dark, glittering water of the underground lake which filled the cavern.

Léon rowed them slowly towards the centre of the lake, and Jessica saw that the rock walls glistened damply, shimmering in the light from the overhead lamps so that the whole vast cavern somehow seemed alive. And from the black shadows at the very back of the cavern, she could hear the sound of tumbling water, a cascade of sound which echoed round and round the vast, enclosed space.

'It was my father who first discovered this place,' Léon told her, his own voice somehow sounding more resonant in this underground fantasy world. 'When I was a child, we used to come down here together and explore it with torches.'

'Who installed the lights?' she asked.

'I did. That's why I wanted to come down here today, to make sure they were working satisfactorily.'

Jessica glanced around a little nervously. 'What if there's a power failure, and the lights go out?' She definitely didn't fancy being in this place in the dark.

'I keep a couple of torches in a waterproof box at the back of the cavern,' he assured her.

'Installing all these lights must have cost a small fortune. Why did you do it?'

'I'll explain that later. First of all, there's something I want to show you.'

He began rowing again, taking them towards the very back of the cavern. The sound of rushing water grew louder, and Jessica twisted her head round, trying to see where it was coming from.

'Over there,' said Léon, directing her gaze.

Her eyes followed his pointing finger, then she gave a small gasp of pure delight as she caught the glitter of water cascading down through the semi-darkness.

'It's a waterfall!' she exclaimed. 'An underground waterfall.'

And so it was, the water tumbling down from high above them, rushing over dark, glistening rocks to a small pool far below, then frothing through a narrow channel to join the main underground lake.

Léon stood up, and Jessica stared at him with sudden nervousness as the boat rocked a little precariously.

'What are you doing?'

'Just coming to sit beside you for a couple of minutes,' he answered, and he settled himself comfortably on the wooden seat. Jessica suddenly didn't feel so relaxed any more. The seat was fairly small, they had to sit close together in order for them both to fit on to it. Why couldn't he have just stayed at his own end of the boat?

'Er—you were going to tell me why you installed the lights,' she reminded him, hoping he couldn't hear the slightly edgy note that had crept into her voice.

'I did it because I'm thinking of opening the cavern to the public. I intend to try and attract tourists to this area,' he answered her.

'Tourists?' she yelped, instantly forgetting all her nervousness. 'Are you mad? This part of France is like a little bit of paradise. Why on earth do you want to bring a lot of noisy, messy tourists here to spoil everything?'

'It might seem like paradise to you and me. But to most of the people who live here, it's an area of low incomes and almost non-existent employment opportunities. The young people have to move away to the cities to get jobs, and the older ones who remain behind have a pretty poor standard of living. The village of Sévignac might look quaint and picturesque to an outsider, but several of the houses are already empty, and more people are going to move out if some new source of income isn't found for them.'

'But *tourists*!' repeated Jessica in dismay.

'Would you prefer a factory or an industrial complex built right here in the valley?' demanded Léon. 'Because that would be about the only other source of new jobs.'

'Well, I suppose if you put it like that——' she conceded very reluctantly.

'Nothing's definite yet,' Léon told her. 'We're still exploring possibilities. At the moment, we're thinking in terms of a small hotel in Sévignac itself, with a well supervised camping and caravan site at the far end of the valley. We're aiming for a steady flow of tourists, not an absolute avalanche. The main problem is finding a specific attraction that'll draw them here. There's the vineyard, of course, we can offer people a tour of the fields and cellars, with a local guide to explain exactly how the wine's made—and a free wine-tasting included, of course,' he added drily. 'Pony-trekking's another possibility, and the river itself could be used for canoeing and swimming. But I'm hoping that opening this cavern to the public will prove a big draw. People seem to enjoy pottering around in caves, and the cavern looks fairly spectacular now it's illuminated.'

'Yes, it does,' agreed Jessica slowly. 'But I can think of something that would be an even bigger draw.'

Léon's black brows drew together. 'You can? What?'

'Opening the château itself. People would flock to see it, I know they would.'

'No!' Léon's response was immediate, and totally adamant.

'But why not?' argued Jessica. 'It would be a bigger attraction than all the other things put together, can't you see that?'

'Of course I can see it,' he growled, 'but the answer's still no. The château's my home, I won't have people tramping in and out of it as if they own it!'

'Not even for just one day a week?' she persisted, reluctant to give up a good idea without a fight. Then, seeing the implacable expression on his face, she frowned and said, 'Why not, Léon?'

He hesitated for a while, and she had the impression that he didn't want to talk about it, that it was too personal. Eventually, though, he lifted his head a little and said in an even voice, 'When I was young—when my mother was alive—the château was my whole world. It was a marvellous place for a child to grow up, I never wanted to leave it. Then my mother died, and after that it became a refuge, a place full of precious memories. In a way, it was even more important to me then; I suppose it represented the security of my childhood. Can you understand that?' Her throat suddenly tight, Jessica nodded. 'But then my father remarried,' Léon went on, his black brows drawing together fiercely at the memory, 'and suddenly the château wasn't my home any longer, it belonged to Celestine. She took it over, changed it beyond all recognition. I felt as if there wasn't a place for me there any more. As soon as I was old enough, I left and I only came back for brief visits, to see my father.'

Jessica looked at him with troubled eyes. 'Your uncle Claude told me what else my mother did,' she admitted in a low voice.

Léon's eyes instantly flared with hard annoyance.

'He had no right telling you that!' Then some of the tension left him again, she saw his rigid muscles relax just a fraction. 'Not that I suppose it's really important any more. Celestine's dead, my father's dead, and now the château's mine I've finally got my home back again. And

I don't intend to share it with anyone—and certainly not with marauding hordes of tourists! I'm sorry if that sounds selfish, but I can't help it, that's the way I feel.'

His possessive tone of voice when he spoke about the château made Jessica bristle slightly, and some of her instinctive sympathy for him drained away.

'Only half of the château's yours,' she reminded him. 'What if I decided to open *my* half to the public? I'm perfectly entitled to do that, aren't I?'

He turned to face her, and the lights overhead shone down full on to his dark features, allowing her to see the tight line of his mouth, the warning glitter in his eyes.

'I don't think I'd pursue that particular idea any further, if I were you,' he warned softly, and there was something in his tone that sent a cascade of goose-pimples racing right down her spine. She had no intention of allowing him to intimidate her, though, so she straightened her shoulders and stared right back at him.

'Why not?' she challenged. 'Aren't I allowed to have any ideas and opinions of my own? The fact that I own half the château means that, to some extent, I'm going to be involved in this project of yours. After all, that's why you brought me here, isn't it? Why you showed me this cavern, and explained what you're planning? I can hardly *not* be involved, under the circumstances.'

'Yes, you're involved,' he agreed tightly. 'It's unfortunate, but it can't be helped. But that doesn't give you the right to walk in and start throwing your weight around.'

'Then exactly what rights do I have?' she demanded.

'None, as far as I can see,' Léon informed her calmly.

'Charming!' Her temper suddenly flared, as it so often seemed to when she was around this infuriating man, and she began to struggle to her feet, giving into a surging impulse to get away from him.

'What do you think you're doing?' asked Léon reasonably.

'I'm getting out of here!'

'How?'

His simple question reminded her that they were sitting in a rowing-boat in the middle of an underground lake. Her temper subsided as quickly as it had flared up and, beginning to feel distinctly foolish, she rather sulkily subsided back into the boat.

'Your trouble, Jessica, is that you far too often act on impulse,' he told her.

'I don't need a lecture,' she muttered. 'And certainly not from you.'

'No, perhaps you don't,' he conceded thoughtfully. Something in his tone made her glance up, and she was disconcerted to find that he had begun to look at her in a rather disturbing manner. 'I wonder exactly what you do want from me?' he went on in that same reflective tone.

'Nothing. Absolutely nothing,' she assured him hastily, hoping he couldn't hear the slightly nervous edge to her voice.

'Are you sure? Sometimes when we're together, I get the impression——' His voice trailed away and, seeing the speculative expression in his eyes, Jessica jumped in rather too hurriedly.

'Whatever impression you're getting, it's the wrong one! You don't even like me. Remember, Léon? I'm Celestine's daughter, I've grabbed a large chunk of your inheritance. You don't *like* me,' she repeated, her eyes huge now with sudden apprehension.

But he was still looking at her with those black, all-seeing eyes, and for the first time she realised it was cold inside the cavern. She had begun to shiver, tiny shudders running through her body in steady waves.

'When we first met, every time I looked at you all I could see was Celestine,' he agreed, after a moment's silence. 'You're so like her physically that I couldn't believe you weren't like her in other ways as well. But you're not. You're a person in your own right. And that person is starting to interest me,' he finished softly.

'Oh, you don't want to be interested in me,' she gabbled with growing edginess. 'I'm dull, really dull, you'd be bored to death if you spent too much time with me.'

'Do you think so?' Léon's brows drew together. 'Apparently you're not only impulsive, you've also got a giant-sized inferiority complex. Where did you get it from, Jessica? Some man who walked out on you, convinced you that you weren't worth loving?'

And that was just a little too near the truth for comfort. Jessica dragged in a deep, unsteady breath, then forced herself to laugh, as if she found his question deeply amusing.

'So now we're talking about loving, are we? Really, Léon, you do seem to be running through the whole gamut of emotions this afternoon. And I thought you were such a cold man, that you didn't have any feelings at all. Or if you did, you kept them locked away where no one could ever see them.'

That seemed to strike home just as deeply as the perceptive remark which he had made. They stared at each other warily, both briefly silent, then Léon's mouth relaxed into a slow and yet somehow disturbing smile.

'*Touché*,' he said softly. 'We seem to be well matched. Do you suppose we would strike sparks off each other in other ways as well?'

Against her will, Jessica found herself remembering

the kiss he had given her on the day they had visited the vineyard. Something inside her began to feel as if it wanted to slowly melt, but she wouldn't let it; she had already decided that she just wasn't going to let herself get involved. This man wasn't like Steven, she had already realised that he was far, far more dangerous. If she was ever crazy enough to let him inside her defences, then she wouldn't just walk away hurt when it was all over, she could all too easily end up permanently crippled. And she definitely didn't intend to let that happen.

Only it was a little difficult to keep her distance from him in this ridiculously cramped boat, especially when he was sitting so close beside her and seemed to be showing no inclination to move. In fact, he had even edged a little nearer, she could feel the warmth of him all down the right side of her body, and there was no way she could get away from him, not without going over the side of the boat.

For a moment, she even contemplated that drastic step. She was a good swimmer, she could easily make it out of the cave and back to the river bank. Then common sense stepped in, and she silently laughed at herself. This wasn't some Victorian melodrama, she wasn't about to be ravished against her will. Anyway, that was probably an impossibility in this tiny little boat!

Feeling more confident, she sat up straight and looked calmly at Léon.

'Hadn't we better be getting back?' she suggested.

'No, I don't think so,' he answered, equally coolly. 'Not yet.'

Her skin began to prickle all over again. 'Er—why not?' she asked cautiously.

Léon gave a sudden wolfish smile. 'You had just

decided that you were perfectly safe with me, hadn't you?' he told her with lazy amusement. 'But you're wrong, Jessica. I don't think you've been safe since the day I scooped you up and carried you out of that burning theatre.'

She cleared her throat nervously. 'Léon, I don't want——'

Her voice trailed away as his arm slid casually around her shoulder.

'Yes, you *do* want,' he informed her slightly huskily. 'But for some reason, you're afraid. Ever since we met, you've been a litle frightened of me. And I think I'm beginning to understand why. It's because we react to each other. If I touch you like this—' his finger trailed lightly down her bare arm '—then we both feel the same thing.'

Jessica yawned rather ostentatiously. 'Then what you're feeling right now is boredom.'

'Really?' came his mocking reply, one black eyebrow shooting sky-high. 'Then I must have spent a large proportion of my adult life feeling—bored.'

Jessica had the uneasy feeling that this conversation was starting to get right out of hand. And the trouble was, she didn't know what to do about it. She ran her fingers a little uneasily through her dark, tousled curls, then decided that it would probably be best to tackle the problem head-on.

'All right,' she said bluntly. 'What exactly do you want from me?'

Léon looked at her speculatively. 'I think—yes, I think,' he mused thoughtfully, 'that I would rather like to kiss you again. To see if last time was just a fluke.'

'Last time?' she echoed politely, as if she couldn't even remember the occasion.

He shook his head in obvious amusement. 'Poor acting, Jessica.'

She felt herself flushing slightly, but thought—fervently hoped—that he couldn't see it in the shadowy light that filled the cavern. In fact, the whole thing was starting to feel rather like a bad dream. The small boat rocking gently on the underground lake, the tumbling waterfall behind them, the dark, glistening walls—and the suddenly too-familiar face of the man beside her. Only he wasn't beside her now, he was leaning over her, his features standing out with vivid clarity. The diamond-hard eyes, the black hair, that jagged scar——

Then he bent his head a little further, but he didn't kiss her mouth, as she had been expecting. Instead his lips trailed down the side of her neck in a featherlight touch, making her shudder involuntarily.

'Mm, nice,' he murmured appreciatively. 'I rather thought that it might be.'

'Now that's over, can we go?' she said stiffly.

'Over?' he repeated. 'But Jessica, we haven't even started yet. In fact, we've barely touched on the preliminaries.'

'As far as I'm concerned, this is as far as we go,' she retorted, then was a little dismayed to find that he wasn't angry, in fact he was smiling again. Why did that smile of his unnerve her so much?

'I think we'll just carry on until you're not frightened of me any more,' he told her, as if she didn't have—had never had—any say in the matter.

'I am *not* frightened of you,' she announced with a touch of exasperation.

'Then why won't you kiss me?' he responded, perfectly reasonably.

'Because—because I don't even like you!'

'Children used to get beaten for telling such whopping lies,' he warned, his black eyes glinting with clear amusement. 'All right, there was a time when we didn't get along too well. But that was probably my fault, I wasn't particularly pleasant to you when we first met. I told you, for a while I couldn't separate you from your mother in my mind. But I can tell the difference now. Very clearly,' he added meaningfully.

What was he up to? The question whizzed round and round inside Jessica's head. He wanted something, this elaborate game was all leading up to something, she could sense it—and she instinctively knew that she wasn't going to like it, whatever it turned out to be. He was playing with her, all this business of wanting to kiss her was just a blind, there was an ulterior motive lurking under that teasing, charming façade. She had better be careful, very, very careful. This man was extremely clever—and probably also extremely devious. If only she didn't find his nearness *quite* so disturbing. And if only they weren't stuck in this damned boat!

He bent his head a little again so that his mouth hovered tantalisingly close to hers. Jessica fought back another rash of goose-pimples. This would be a lot easier to cope with if the man weren't so wickedly attractive, she told herself a little grimly. Then there wasn't time to tell herself anything more, or to make any plans on how to cope with the situation, because he had evidently got tired of waiting. Without any warning, his mouth abruptly closed over hers, and he finally carried out his threat to kiss her.

And a very thorough kiss it was, too. His lips moved gently but expertly, his tongue knew exactly when to probe a little further, when to hold back, skilfully tantalising before setting out on a fresh and sweet trail of

exploration. Perhaps it was that cool expertise that
helped her to keep her head, chilled her slightly, left her
surprisingly untouched. She felt as if she knew exactly
how this man would make love, always on his own terms,
dictating the pace, the rhythm, even the timing of his
partner's final response.

Léon at last lifted his head.

'I enjoyed it more last time,' he murmured.

'Perhaps that's because it wasn't planned,' came her
low mutter.

'You think this lacks spontaneity? Perhaps you're
right,' he said thoughtfully. 'We spent far too much time
talking about it. The final event was almost bound to be
an anticlimax. What do you think we should do about it?'

'I think we should just forget the whole thing and get
back to the château,' she said a little tartly.

'Perhaps you're right——' he mused, to her great
relief.

Jessica slumped back on the seat and slowly began to
relax. It looked as if this dangerous confrontation was
finally over, and she started to congratulate herself on
getting through it relatively unscathed. In fact, she was
so pleased with the way she had kept her head, that she
stopped paying any attention to Léon, and so she was
totally unprepared for the silent assault that followed.

Afterwards, she couldn't have explained to anyone
exactly how it had happened. One moment she had been
sitting there feeling rather smug at the way she had got
through these difficult few minutes without too much
damage to her nervous system, the next Léon's lips were
on hers and the world had turned into a dark, whirling
place where reality had retreated, swept away by a whole
torrent of new and totally disturbing sensations.

It wasn't anything like the kisses he had given her

before: there was no control, no expertise, just a relentless pursuit of pleasure as he probed and nibbled and explored with a casual disregard for anything except his own enjoyment. Only, to her amazement, it was somehow her enjoyment too. She didn't understand it, but she seemed to feel his pleasure as intensely as her own, every jolt of delight doubled in intensity because it was shared.

Vague memories of wanting to fight him drifted into her head. Then they drifted straight out again. She couldn't hold on to any thought for more than a couple of seconds, he wouldn't let her, he was forcing her to abandon all logic, all common sense, somersaulting her headlong into an entirely different dimension that acknowledged nothing but the senses, and the multitude of different sensations they were capable of experiencing.

Through the thundering in her ears, she faintly heard him give a small grunt of satisfaction. Then his clever fingers slid down, her skin quivered under his touch as he dealt quickly, efficiently, with the small buttons that fastened the bodice of her sundress.

Struggling to make sense of what was happening, she caught hold of his wrists with some confused intention of pushing away those lethally experienced hands. It was the first time she had ever touched him voluntarily, and the instant her fingers closed over him she knew she had made a deadly mistake: she couldn't let go, her hands were locked on to him and she was somehow pulling him closer instead of trying to fight free.

'I don't understand——' she murmured in real distress.

'There's nothing to understand,' Léon told her softly, 'just let yourself *feel*——'

The last button smoothly parted company with the last buttonhole, the thin cotton fell away and he swiftly moved in to claim the soft swell of her breast for his own. His touch was unexpectedly light, exploring the outer perimeters with almost lazy strokes before just one finger slid over the full underswell to rest very gently on the central peak. Then the warm finger moved away again almost instantly, so that she wasn't quite sure if she had imagined the deep pulse of pleasure that had shot through her.

And Jessica gradually allowed herself to relax, hardly realising that she had instinctively tensed herself against pain, her body vividly remembering how Steven's fingers had dug so deeply into her softness that the bruises had lasted for days, how he had squeezed and manipulated, muttering breathlessly, telling her how much she was liking it and not seeming to know—or care—that all she was experiencing was a deep hurt and a painful emptiness.

And all the time it could have been like this sweet spiral of delight that was trailing in the wake of Léon's fingers; fingers which weren't digging, weren't pinching, were just drifting in an exquisite series of caresses as he moved slowly but inexorably back towards the central core.

Then for an instant he paused, she felt him draw in a light breath, as if something were troubling him, distracting him.

'When I first touched you, you flinched,' he said quietly. 'You thought I was going to hurt you. Who taught you to expect pain?'

Jessica's mouth was suddenly dry. 'He didn't mean to,' she muttered. 'He was just—careless.'

Leon swore softly but vehemently under his breath. 'I

won't be careless,' he promised, and there was a slightly
hard note in his voice now, as if he was very angry about
something. Then he bent his dark head, and an instant
later his tongue very softly touched the aching peak
where his finger had rested only moments ago, licking
warmly but with purposeful gentleness, as if he were
determined to lick away all memory of pain. But it wasn't
necessary for him to be gentle, for Jessica had already
forgotten all about Steven, had forgotten just about
everything as small starbursts of pleasure exploded under
her skin, ignited by the wickedly exciting rasp of his
tongue.

Then an ice-cold splash against her bare, heated skin
made her gasp. She half lifted her head just in time to feel
a second shower of icy droplets hit her.

Leon stared at her ruefully. 'It's dripping down from
the roof,' he told her slightly apologetically. 'One
disadvantage of trying to make love in a damp cave.' He
leaned forward and licked the water off her skin. 'Mm,
cool and fresh,' he murmured. 'But it doesn't taste as
delicious as you do.'

Jessica blinked hard, as if she had just woken up from
a weird and exotic dream. The cave, the underground
lake slowly zoomed back into focus, then she stared down
at her own half-naked body, as if trying to figure out just
how she had got like that. There was a small knot of
panic building up inside her stomach now, she could only
seem to half remember what had happened. She had a
strong presentiment of danger, though; she was getting
into a situation that she just didn't know how to handle,
and given half a chance it would lead to—to what?

It was a question she definitely didn't want to answer.
And the sense of panic was growing stronger all the time,
all she wanted now was to get away. Only she couldn't,

something—someone—was stopping her.

She lifted her gaze and found herself staring straight into Léon's glittering black eyes; then she felt his hand linked around her wrist in a light grip, and she immediately began to struggle.

'Jessica, don't be stupid——' he began reasonably, but she was suddenly deaf to reason, she simply struggled even harder. 'Jessica, stop it!'

His arm started to go round her, as if to restrain her, and she lunged to one side, determined to avoid him. The small boat rocked precariously, and Léon shouted a warning, but she was hopelessly off balance now. She fell heavily against the side of the boat, which promptly turned over, tipping them both into the water.

It was freezing! The cold, more than anything, finally knocked some sense back into Jessica's confused head, and as she surfaced, spluttering and coughing, she remembered her behaviour of a few moments ago with a mixture of wonder and shame. What on earth had made her over-react so strongly? All right, so Léon's love-making had threatened to get rather out of hand, but that had really been no excuse for her to go over the top like that. Why did she get in such a panic whenever this man was around? And where *was* he? She began to glance around in alarm; the upturned boat was floating nearby, but apart from that the water was calm and undisturbed. There was no sign of Léon.

She was just about to dive down in a frantic effort to find him when his dark head silently surfaced just a couple of feet away, his hair sleekly glued to his head, his black gaze swivelling round to fix on her steadily.

Jessica swallowed hard. He was wet and cold, and he was no doubt going to be angry—very, very angry. It was all his fault, of course: if he hadn't insisted on kissing her then it would never have happened, but she had the feeling he wasn't going to look at it quite like that.

Léon continued to tread water and to look at her in that disturbingly thoughtful manner.

'I suppose that was one fairly effective way of dampening my ardour,' he remarked at last, his voice astonishingly calm. 'I can think of several less drastic ways, though.'

She stared at him suspiciously. 'Why aren't you shouting at me?'

His black eyebrows lifted expressively. 'Is that what you want me to do? Would that make you feel less guilty about dumping me in the water?'

'I do *not* feel guilty,' she threw back at him furiously. 'It's no more than you deserve.'

His eyebrows shot even higher. 'For simply kissing you?' He actually seemed amused now.

'You didn't just—just kiss me,' Jessica spluttered.

'I don't recall it going very much further than that,' he mused. 'If it had, I'm sure I would have remembered it. And of course, we were in a small and fairly unstable rowing-boat. That in itself must have kept our options pretty limited.'

Jessica glared at him furiously. 'I wish you'd drowned!' she yelled.

A lazy grin touched the corners of his mouth. 'Sorry to disappoint you. Can you swim?'

'Of course I can swim.'

'I'll see you back at the château, then,' Léon told her calmly.

And with that, he set off towards the cave entrance in a powerful crawl.

It was a couple of minutes before Jessica began to

follow in his wake, splashing along a lot more slowly and less elegantly. And once her brief burst of temper began to die away, other more disturbing thoughts moved in to take its place.

Once more, she had the powerful impression that Léon Castillon was playing a game with her. But he wasn't simply amusing himself, it was a game with a purpose, although he was the only one who knew what that purpose might be. She had already realised that was the reason she was scared of him: she was sure he was using her, manipulating her, in order to get something that he wanted.

And she nervously wondered just how far he would go to achieve his ultimate aim—and how long it would be before she discovered exactly what that aim was.

CHAPTER SIX

As she plodded slowly back to the château, dripping a trail of water behind her, Jessica very much hoped no one would see her in her present condition. It might be just a little difficult to explain why she was soaking wet from head to toe. Then, despite everything that had happened, she gave a faint grin as she realised that Léon would be facing the same problem. Of course, he knew the château and the grounds like the back of his hand, so he was probably finding it much easier to sneak in without being seen.

Jessica was taking the path which she and Léon had taken earlier, trudging along steadily as it wound its way steeply up the high outcrop of rock, then following it through the gardens to the château itself. She figured she would creep in through one of the back entrances. That way, there was less chance of being seen than if she just marched straight in through the front door.

The back entrance was in sight now, and she released a sigh of relief. She was just about to sprint over the last few yards when something moved to her left, making her turn her head. A second later, she groaned silently. Sitting in a straight-backed chair in a sheltered corner of the terrace that overlooked the garden was Léon's grandmother!

Despite the bright sunshine, she was dressed exactly the same as the last time Jessica had seen her, covered in black from head to toe. Very appropriate, thought Jessica wryly. Like some high executioner!

His grandmother stared down at her with those black, all-seeing eyes that bore such an uncanny resemblance to Léon's.

'You're wet,' she remarked succinctly.

'Yes, I am,' agreed Jessica, determined not to volunteer any more information than she absolutely had to.

His grandmother's thin mouth narrowed a little further. 'I have just seen Léon. He is also wet.'

'Good heavens!' said Jessica sweetly. 'What a coincidence.'

The black eyes became even more distant. 'I don't like insolence. Your mother was always very insolent.'

Small wonder, if you spoke to her in the same way that you speak to me, thought Jessica furiously. But she said nothing out loud, for she had no intention of getting into a slanging match with this sharp-tongued old woman. And for the first time, she felt a brief but unexpectedly sharp flash of sympathy for her mother. She was beginning to realise that it couldn't have been easy for her, living here with these arrogant Castillons. André might have been besotted with her, but it was pretty clear that the rest of them hadn't had much time for her.

The black gaze was fixed on her again now. 'How much longer do you suppose you'll be staying here at the château?' enquired Léon's grandmother.

'I've absolutely no idea,' answered Jessica, with deliberate wide-eyed innocence. 'But to be honest, I'm beginning to like it here so much that I might just stay indefinitely.'

The old lady snorted in disgust, and Jessica suddenly felt much more cheerful. One point to me, she thought with a grin.

'I think I'd better go inside and change,' she went on.

Then she added, a little mischievously, 'Was Léon *very* wet?'

His grandmother stared down at her with those fierce, black eyes. 'I'm sure that you know exactly how wet he was. Don't try and play your tawdry little games with me, young lady. Léon might be dazzled by a pretty face and body, but I can see you only too clearly.'

'I'm sure that Léon is never dazzled by anyone or anything', Jessica retorted a trifle acidly.

'Léon's as likely as his father to be a fool over a woman,' pronounced his grandmother. 'And if you're anything like your mother, you won't hesitate to take advantage of that fact.'

Jessica felt the last of her cheerfulness abruptly evaporate. 'You really are an extremely unpleasant old woman,' she said, in a slightly choked voice. 'And I should think you're probably very lonely as well. After all, who'd want to come and visit you when they know they're only going to get insults slung at them?'

And with that, she whirled round and marched into the château, blazingly angry and yet with a humiliating prickling at the back of her eyes. She rubbed them furiously. Too much sun, she told herself forcefully, it always made her eyes ache and water.

After a shower and a change of clothes, she felt calmer, more in control. All the same, she didn't feel up to facing any of the Castillons again today, and a little later she rang down to the housekeeper and asked if she could have her evening meal in her room.

Next morning, she still felt unaccountably rattled. To her relief, though, she found that Léon intended to ride over to the vineyard, and would be there for most of the day. She lurked behind one of the windows, to make sure that he had actually gone, and gave a sigh of relief when she finally saw him cantering off on his huge black stallion. Like some damned knight on a charger, she told herself scornfully. And yet there was nothing really medieval about Léon, he was very much a man of the twentieth century. On one of her explorations of the château, she had inadvertently opened the door of the room he used as his office, and had stood there goggle-eyed for a couple of minutes, staring at the sophisticated electronic equipment packed into the room. She hadn't even recognised some of it, let alone known how to use it.

Fascinated and impressed, she hadn't heard Léon come up behind her.

'Snooping?' he had enquired softly.

She had jumped violently, then made a valiant attempt to pull herself together.

'Just exploring. I didn't know this was your office.'

'Want to see inside?' he had invited, relenting a little. And before she could refuse, he had swept her in and taken her on an extensive tour of all the machines and gadgets, explaining how they worked and the purpose for which he used them.

Most of it was fairly technical and went straight over her head, but she was left with the overall impression that all these machines helped Léon to make a great deal of money.

'This is my favourite toy,' he had concluded, stopping at the computer console and running his fingers lightly over the keys. 'At the moment, I'm working on a program that will help to predict the general movement of certain shares over a six-month period.'

'Is that possible?' she had asked uncertainly.

Unexpectedly, he had smiled. 'I don't know. Ask me again this time next year.' Then he had caught hold of her shoulders and propelled her towards the door. 'Now, out you go. I've got work to do.'

And she had found herself standing in the corridor,

with the door firmly closing behind her.

Jessica frowned a little as she watched the man on the horse disappearing through the arched entrance to the courtyard. She was very much aware that Léon was starting to confuse her; he was a man of so many contradictions. She never knew what to expect each time she met him, what kind of a mood she would find him in, what his attitude towards her would be.

And she was ready to admit that his attitude of the last couple of days was starting to be distinctly worrying. It was a relief to be free of him for a few hours; perhaps by the time she next saw him she would have sorted it all out in her mind, be more capable of dealing with this man who had crashed into her life only days ago, and succeeded in turning it completely upside down.

Yet perversely, now that he had gone for a few hours and she should have been able to relax, instead she felt restless; she wandered aimlessly through the château and couldn't settle to anything. In the end, getting impatient with herself, she dug a paperback out of her suitcase. She searched the garden to make sure that Léon's grandmother wasn't lurking in a shady corner, then stretched out on the grass for a good read.

By early evening, Léon still hadn't returned. Jessica decided she would have an early night. The book she had picked up had turned out to be surprisingly riveting, she would take it to bed with her and try to finish it.

She had just finished showering when she heard the distinctive sound of a horse's hoofs clattering across the cobbles of the courtyard. Just in time, she stopped herself from rushing across to the window to peer out. It was of no interest to her if he was back or not, she told herself rather crossly, and she picked up her book and hopped into bed.

The light knock on her door came after she had read

only a couple of pages. Annoyed at the interruption, she reluctantly put down the book; then, grumbling softly under her breath, she scrambled out of bed and went over to open the door.

When she saw Léon standing on the other side, her heart gave a funny little skipped beat. Then all her defences flew back into place again, and she frowned darkly at him.

'Do you know what time it is?' she demanded.

'Of course,' he answered smoothly. 'It's just gone eight o'clock.'

'Oh——' she said, a little deflated. She had thought it was much later than that. 'Well, you've still disturbed me. I was in bed.'

'So I see. My God,' he went on, staring at her almost reverently, 'do you really wear those every night?'

Jessica looked down at her plain cotton pyjamas. 'What's wrong with them?'

His black eyebrows shot up expressively. 'Do you really need me to tell you? If you do, certain aspects of your education have been sadly lacking.'

'They're very practical,' Jessica insisted staunchly. 'Anyway, it's absolutely no business of yours what I wear in bed.'

He gave a non-committal shrug which she somehow found strangely worrying. Rather pointedly, she yawned. 'I'm tired, I want to go back to bed. Whatever you want, we can talk about it in the morning.'

'You can't possibly be tired this early in the evening,' he told her calmly. 'And yes, there is something I want to talk to you about. But first, I want to show you something. Have you got a dressing-gown?'

'No. But I don't need one,' she added immediately. 'I'm not going anywhere with you, not tonight.'

Léon regarded her thoughtfully. 'There are times when

you can be irritatingly argumentative.'

'And there are times when *you* can be extremely unreasonable,' she retorted. 'You come knocking on my door in the middle of the night——'

'Eight o'clock in the evening is hardly the middle of the night!'

'Well, maybe not,' she conceded. 'But you don't seriously expect me to go traipsing off with you in my pyjamas, do you?'

To her astonishment, he threw back his head and roared with laughter.

'Jessica, do you seriously suppose that anyone in their right mind is going to try and seduce you while you're wearing those—those——' Words seemed to fail him as he tried to find some way of describing her nightwear. To her utter fury, she found herself turning bright scarlet.

'I never said that you were going to try and—and seduce me,' she muttered angrily.

Léon finally stopped laughing, and with an effort got control of himself again.

'Perhaps we ought to try and start this conversation all over again,' he suggested. 'With luck, we'll make a better job of it the second time.'

'But I don't want to talk to you at all,' she insisted. 'I just want to go to bed—to sleep,' she added hurriedly as she saw a mocking gleam flicker briefly in his black eyes.

'I've been thinking about you today,' he told her, showing absolutely no inclination to leave. 'I began to wonder about your reasons for coming here to the château.'

Jessica stiffened a little. 'I would have thought they were pretty obvious. If someone left you a half-share in a magnificent old château, wouldn't you want to see it?'

'But you didn't even know it was magnificent before you got here,' he pointed out. 'In fact, you didn't ask any questions about it at all. So I began to think that perhaps you had another reason for wanting to rush straight here and see it.'

'What kind of reason?' she asked warily.

'It occurred to me that perhaps you were curious to see the place where your mother had lived for so many years.'

Jessica was just about to deny it emphatically when she suddenly stopped and gave a funny little sigh. 'I suppose you're right,' she said at last with some reluctance. 'Although I honestly don't know why I was so eager to come here. You know what my mother was like, Léon. In fact, you probably understand better than anyone in the world. So why did I suddenly start wanting to know more about her? After all, she certainly never gave a damn about *me*. It doesn't make any sense.'

'It makes sense to me. Most children want to know about their parents, no matter how negligent or unkind those parents may have been.' He let his dark gaze rest on her thoughtfully. 'Won't you come with me, Jessica?' he asked again in an unexpectedly quiet voice. 'There's something I want to show you—something that might help you to get a few things straightened out.'

She hesitated for a few more seconds, then finally gave a small shrug and nodded. She followed him out into the corridor, then let out a small splutter of protest as he casually linked his fingers through her own.

'There's no need for that! I'm not going to run away.'

'I know,' he agreed calmly, but he still didn't let go of her and there was no way she could break free, his fingers were locked too firmly around hers. She kept forgetting how physically strong he was, although she knew that she ought to remember only too well. On the night of the fire, he had carried her with ease, even though she was a tall girl and not exactly a featherweight.

And now he was towing her along in his wake, taking

her to a wing of the château that she had only briefly
explored before, not being able to see very much of it
because most of the doors had been locked. As she
reluctantly trudged along beside him, through the long
corridors, up a flight of winding stairs, then along
another corridor, she wondered what on earth it was that
he was so determined to show her—and why.

At last, he stopped outside an ornately carved door.
Her heart began to thump rather strangely, and all of a
sudden she knew she didn't really want to see what was
on the other side. It was too late, though; Léon had
already taken a key from his pocket and was unlocking
the door. Then it swung open, and he gently pushed her
inside.

The sun hadn't quite set yet, and its light filled the
room, clearly illuminating it, so that Jessica could see
every corner. And for several seconds she simply stared
around her, wide-eyed.

Although the rest of the château was elegantly and
very expensively furnished, this room was something else
again. From the incredibly thick pile of the carpet
beneath her bare feet to the silk covers on the bed and the
hand-painted wallpaper, the room shimmered with
blatant luxury. The colour scheme was ice-blue, even in
the glow from the setting sun it radiated coolness, and
Jessica felt as if she was standing in the centre of some
magnificent ice cavern.

'Do you like it?' asked Léon quietly.

'It's stunning,' she said slowly. 'Although I'm not sure I
actually *like* it. It's a bit——'

'Over the top?' he suggested.

'Something like that,' she agreed, with a wry grimace.

'That shouldn't really surprise you,' he told her. 'I
thought you would have realised by now that your mother
never believed in doing things by half-measures.'

'My mother——?' Jessica's voice trailed away, and she looked at the room with new eyes. She supposed she should have realised it straight away, for who else at the Château de Sévignac would ever have decorated a room so extravagantly?

She took a couple of steps forward, and for a moment allowed her imagination a free rein. Her mother had sat at that gilded dressing-table as she had brushed her hair, painted on her make-up, had sunk her bare toes into the sensually soft pile of the carpet just as Jessica was doing right now, had slept in that incredibly luxurious bed with its silk covers, velvet drapes and the pillows trimmed with hand-made lace. This room, with its unashamed luxury and yet its hint of coldness, gave her the first real clue she had had to the true essence of Celestine Castillon.

'Look to your right,' instructed Léon, his voice so close that she realised he had silently come up behind her and was now standing only inches away. 'You haven't yet seen what I brought you here to see.'

Jessica wasn't sure that she wanted to see any more, but Léon's hands were on her shoulders now, he was propelling her round so that she no longer had any choice.

She found she was facing an ornate fireplace. Delicate porcelain figures graced the mantelpiece, and there was a finely-chased silver candelabra as a centrepiece, but she didn't notice them, her gaze had already raced upwards to the large painting that hung above it.

It was an incredibly detailed, brilliantly executed portrait. The white folds of the woman's dress, the heavy gold chain that hung around her throat, the dark jewel glinting in the ring on her finger all seemed real enough to touch. Jessica scarcely saw them, though. Her eyes were fixed on the woman's face, the pale, perfect skin, the dark, knowing gaze, and the sweep of the gleaming black hair. And the faint smile on those exquisitely shaped lips.

For the first time, Jessica knew what her mother had really looked like. The blurred snapshot she had found after Aunt Lettie had died had given no more than a vague indication of an attractive woman. Jessica had certainly had no idea Celestine had been so incredibly lovely, and she gazed up at the portrait now almost in disbelief.

At last she knew what Léon and Claude had meant when they had said André Castillon had been besotted. This woman—her mother, she reminded herself a little disbelievingly—would surely have had the power to dazzle just about anyone.

'She was beautiful, wasn't she?' said Léon softly in her ear. 'On the outside, at least.'

'Why did you want me to see this picture?' asked Jessica in a rather queer voice.

'I thought it might help you to put things in perspective,' Léon answered, after a brief pause. 'And I particularly wanted you to see things clearly tonight.'

Something in his tone dragged Jessica out of her preoccupation with the painting, and she slowly turned round to face him.

'Why?' she said warily. 'What's so special about tonight?'

Léon gave her that lazy smile with which she was becoming so familiar, and which was starting to send small tendrils of warmth through her every time she saw it.

'Because tonight seemed as good a time as any to propose to you.'

'To *what*?' Jessica gaped at him. She couldn't believe he had actually just said that.

'To propose,' he repeated very calmly. 'I think it would be an excellent idea if you and I were married. I've discussed it today with Claude——'

'Oh, you've discussed it with Claude, have you?' she broke in furiously. 'I suppose you've discussed it with just about everyone—except with me.'

'No, only with Claude,' Léon replied, his voice still cool and steady. 'I always talk over personal matters with him, I deeply value his opinion.'

'Well, you can just go back and tell him that I've absolutely no intention of marrying you,' Jessica retorted, her face brightly flushed now in contrast with Léon's own dark, passive features. 'It's the craziest idea I ever heard of. What on earth made you think I'd ever agree to go along with it?'

Léon shrugged. 'It seemed like a very practical solution to a lot of our problems. Once you've had time to think it over, I'm sure you'll look at it in the same way.'

'All I'm likely to think is that you ought to be certified!' Jessica said, a little grimly. 'Just give me one good reason why I ought to marry you. And don't give me any drivel about being in love with me, either, because I'm not naïve enough to swallow that one!'

Léon's black eyes seemed to go a shade darker, if that was possible.

'No, I'm not in love with you,' he agreed, and for the first time she heard a slight edge to his tone. 'I've never been in love in my life, and I don't intend to be in the future. I saw what love did to my father: it emasculated him, turned him into a man I hardly recognised. But I enjoy *making* love—and I'm certainly not indifferent to you in that respect, Jessica.' His voice had subtly altered, taking on a slightly husky undertone as he spoke those last words, and Jessica felt a small, familiar shiver snake its way up her spine. This man was dangerous, she reminded herself. He probably knew a hundred and one different ways of getting what he wanted—and what he wanted right now was her. She remembered the vivid impression she had had that he was playing some kind of game. Well, she had been right. And now she knew exactly where that game had been leading.

She shivered again, and hoped he hadn't noticed; she didn't want him to know how suddenly vulnerable she felt.

'I don't think that wanting to go to bed with me is any basis for a marriage,' she told him stiffly.

'Of course it isn't,' he agreed immediately, to her astonishment. 'But it's a foundation on which we can build. Think about it, Jessica. You haven't any family or home of your own, you're virtually all alone in the world. All you've got is your dancing career, and that could come to an end at any time. A broken bone, a strained back—dancers are prone to all sorts of injuries. And even if you're lucky and your body holds up, the revue might decide to cancel your contract. Jobs aren't easy to find, you've already discovered that. What I'm offering you is a secure future, with a home and a ready-made family.'

'Some family!' she scoffed, totally unimpressed. 'Your uncle Claude, and your grandmother, who doesn't even like me.'

Léon's eyes glinted briefly, but he quickly brought himself under control again.

'There's also myself,' he reminded her.

Jessica was about to make a very barbed answer, but saw the expression on his face and stopped herself just in time.

'OK,' she said, 'so that's what you're offering *me*. But just what do *you* expect to get out of this marriage?'

He looked a little surprised at her question. 'I would have thought that was perfectly obvious. I get what your mother took away from me—the rest of my inheritance.'

This time, Jessica really did gape at him. 'I don't believe it,' she muttered incredulously at last. 'You'd really marry me just to get your share of the château back again?'

A hint of impatience showed on Léon's dark face. 'Why do you find that so incredible? You must know how important the château is to me, I thought I'd explained that to you very clearly, that you understood. Unless I marry you myself, it's almost certain that you'll one day marry someone else. Then your share of the château will eventually pass to any children of such a marriage, and out of the Castillon family.'

Jessica shook her head slowly. 'I was wrong about you. I thought you were modern and civilised, but you're not, it's all on the surface. Underneath you're still like some medieval overlord, all you're really concerned about is holding on to what's yours, no matter what it takes.'

A dark frown was beginning to gather between Léon's glittering eyes.

'I certainly have a strong sense of family duty, of family responsibility,' he agreed. 'I don't see that there's anything particularly medieval about that. The Château de Sévignac has belonged to the Castillons for generations. I feel it's my duty to try and keep that inheritance intact, ready to pass on to the next generation—to my own son.'

Something stirred deep inside Jessica's stomach. 'Your son?' she croaked. 'You mean——?'

'I mean that this would most certainly be a genuine marriage,' he said sharply. 'And, God willing, we would have children.' The black brows relaxed, his mouth set into a gentler line. 'I think we would have very beautiful children, Jessica,' he murmured persuasively.

To her horror, for a moment she found herself

desperately tempted; she could almost see those children, with the dark hair of their parents and Léon's black, black eyes——

With an enormous effort, she jerked herself back to reality, pushing the vivid visions of the future firmly away from her.

'No,' she whispered. Then, much more decisively, 'No!'

Léon instantly looked displeased, and a small inner tremor shook her as she saw the shadow that settled over his taut features.

'Perhaps you need time to think this over?' he suggested.

'I do *not* need time,' she insisted a little frantically. 'I don't know why you thought I'd ever agree, the whole thing's totally insane.'

'To me, it seems perfectly logical,' Léon retorted. Then he gave a small, placatory gesture. 'Look, Jessica, I've given this a great deal of thought. I wouldn't even have suggested it if I didn't think we could live comfortably together. I'm not so cold-blooded that I could face spending the rest of my life with someone I couldn't get along with, someone who didn't strike some kind of response from me. Yes, we argue at times, but that's healthy, I like women who have their own opinions and are prepared to defend them. And whether you're willing to admit it or not, there *is* a certain empathy between us. I think a marriage such as the one I've proposed would work out entirely satisfactorily. And I believe, once you've calmed down a little, you'll see it that way as well.'

'I'm sure I won't!' she retorted with new spirit, as the utter absurdity of his suggestion hit her all over again. 'It still sounds to me more like a business proposition than a proposal. Marriage should be more—more——'

'More romantic?' suggested Léon, with a small sigh.

'The English always insist that the French are the romantics. But in truth, I think that we have a much more practical approach to life than you do. I agree, though, that marriage should have its more impractical side.' His mouth curled into a sudden smile as the implication of his words hit her, instantly making her flush. 'I don't think that we'll have any trouble with the impracticalities, do you?' he said with velvet smoothness.

Jessica turned her back on him so that he couldn't see her skin had just gone an even brighter shade of scarlet.

'That's something neither of us are going to get the chance to find out,' she declared with rigid determination.

His hands slid over her shoulders again. He didn't try to turn her round, though; instead they just rested there, holding her lightly but firmly, refusing to allow her to escape. And because Jessica didn't want him to think that she was scared of him, that she wasn't perfectly in control of the whole situation, she didn't try to wriggle away but just stood there, gritting her teeth and trying to ignore those two warm patches where his palms were in contact with her body.

'Are you still scared of me?' Léon said softly. 'I won't hurt you. You know that by now.'

'I've never been scared of you,' she insisted stubbornly.

'But I think that you were—perhaps still are,' he went on. 'Was it because of that other man? The one who taught you that lovemaking was painful?' His fingers tightened a little. 'I wish I could meet him,' he growled. 'I'd teach him that women aren't there simply to be abused.'

'He didn't mean it,' Jessica said awkwardly, a little shaken by his sudden vehemence. 'He'd drunk too much, he was just—clumsy.'

'Did you love him?'

The question surprised her. So did Léon's tone of voice, he sounded almost—jealous? she thought, incredulously. No, she had to be mistaken, that just wasn't possible.

'I thought I did at the time,' she said, after a slight pause. 'Now—well, I'm not so sure. I think perhaps I was—rather dazzled by him. I suppose that's not the same thing as love.'

'No, it isn't,' agreed Léon. 'And do you suppose that I'll ever manage to—dazzle you?'

His purring voice succeeded in putting such a wealth of meaning into that one little word that another flush of heat covered her skin. She was so bright red now that she would probably glow in the dark! she thought to herself resentfully, and was thoroughly grateful that she still had her back to him. Although she wished he would let go of her, she was uncomfortably aware of him standing just behind her, only his hands actually in contact with her, but the heat of his body seeming to burn its way right down her back.

'I'm sure you'd be able to dazzle anybody, if you put your mind to it,' she answered a little acidly.

'Then why am I having such trouble convincing you that we would have a very successful marriage?' he asked reasonably.

'Léon, if you mention marriage just once more, I'll—I'll——' She spluttered to a halt, she couldn't think of anything dreadful enough with which to threaten him.

'Very well,' he conceded, 'I shan't say another word on the subject. At least, not tonight,' he continued, just as she was about to heave a huge sigh of relief. 'And of course, I can't promise that I shan't try to persuade you in other ways.'

His hands slid down a little further, then rested against

her passively. Feeling her tense, he went on thoughtfully,
'If you were really scared of me, I think you'd probably
try to run away at this point. But since you insist you're
not frightened, and of course I don't—*dazzle* you, there's
absolutely nothing to be nervous about—is there?'

Jessica clearly heard the note of challenge in his voice.
She gulped silently, then sternly told herself she was quite
capable of coping with this.

'Of course not,' she answered firmly, and was pleased
that her voice didn't even quaver.

His hands shifted an inch lower. 'And you're quite sure
that no matter what I do, I can't change your mind?'

For an instant, her mind flickered back to what had
happened between them in that cavern. Then she
straightened her shoulders again. She knew what to
expect now, she was in no danger. With just a little self-
control, she should be able to deal with this quite easily.
And if she finally succeeded in convincing him that she
was totally indifferent to him, that no matter what he
did, he just didn't turn her on, then perhaps he would
forget all about this ridiculous idea of marriage and
leave her alone.

His hands moved again, resting lightly against her
ribs. He was still making no effort to turn her round to
face him, he seemed content to stand behind her, his
breath warm against her neck, his voice a low murmur in
her ear.

'There are times when it's almost embarrassingly easy
to read your mind, Jessica. You think that all you've got
to do is turn yourself into a frigid little statue and I'll lose
all interest in you. Right?'

'You're the mind-reader!' she retorted stiffly, secretly a
little appalled at the way he always seemed to know
exactly what she was thinking, 'Since you reckon you've
got it all worked out, there's not much point in arguing

with you, is there?'

'Not really,' he agreed amicably. 'But let's go over it just one more time. If I do this—' and his fingers slid round to the front of her body, stopping just under the full swell of her breast '—it doesn't have the slightest effect on you. Have I got it right?'

'You most certainly have,' she insisted through clenched teeth. 'Now drop it, Léon. This whole charade has gone far enough.'

'But I'm still not convinced,' he told her smoothly. 'And I don't think I can drop it until we've settled this thing one way or the other.'

Jessica glanced around a little wildly. His arms were still locked around her, his hands resting lightly but firmly under her ribs, and there was no way she could get away from him without turning the whole thing into an ignominious struggle. Anyway, she argued with herself, the whole point of this exercise was to convince him once and for all that he left her cold, that he could keep this up all night without getting a flicker of response from her.

'All right,' she said, somehow keeping her voice completely steady, 'what exactly do I have to do to get through to you? Make you see that you don't do a thing for me?'

'You don't have to do anything at all,' Léon assured her softly. 'All you have to do is let me carry on a little longer touching you like this—and like this——'

A tiny draught touched her skin and she realised that he had swiftly, expertly undone the buttons on the front of her pyjama jacket, that it had now fallen open, leaving her bare flesh easy prey for those clever hands of his. With a small gasp, she tried to drag it closed again, but it was too late, he was already burrowing deep inside, a small murmur of pleasure sounding in her ear as his fingers closed around the warm swell of her breasts, sliding appreciatively over their perfect shape, teasing the pink tips into a betraying hardness.

'You've got beautiful breasts,' came Léon's slightly husky whisper. 'They were made to be touched, to be caressed. Admit it, Jessica, don't you like it when my hand moves like this—and touches you here?'

One finger lightly grazed its way over her tautly throbbing nipple, and she only just managed to choke back the faint groan of pure pleasure. Don't let him know, she told herself a little frantically, don't let him know!

Although she hadn't the faintest idea how she managed it, she somehow succeeded in keeping her body stiff and unresponsive. There! she thought to herself almost savagely. Let's see how he likes making love to a log!

But to her chagrin, he wasn't put off. Instead, he gave a low, deep chuckle.

'Good try, Jessica. But a couple of things give you away. Your voice is cold, but your skin's hot, burning hot. And if I shift my hand a couple of inches, I can feel your heart thundering away like a drum. But most of all, *ma chérie*, it's those beautiful breasts of yours that tell me the truth.' He swung her round a little. 'See?' he prompted throatily.

She found herself facing a full-length mirror, and shivered uncontrollably as she stared at the reflection which confronted her.

The girl in the mirror was half-naked, the pyjama jacket swinging open to clearly show the fine body underneath, the breasts standing out proudly, the pink tips contracted to a tight, aching hardness. Then Jessica's disturbed gaze drifted to the reflection of the man who stood behind her, his eyes black as midnight on a cloudy, starless night, his dark, strong hands starkly silhouetted against the much lighter colour of her own skin, their two bodies forming a fascinating pattern of shapes and shades.

Léon's breathing wasn't quite so even now, and his hands began to move with new purpose, rubbing themselves against the delicate softness of her skin, setting up a delicious hot friction that seemed to burn all her nerve-ends; then they slid swiftly down, delving beneath the waistband of her pyjama pants, gliding across her firm, flat stomach, totally ignoring her low moan of protest. Her stomach muscles quivered with a queer, unfamiliar tremor of anticipation, a dizzy wave of pleasure swept over her, closely followed by an even stronger wave of a new and totally terrifying need.

'Do you remember what I once told you?' Léon muttered thickly in her ear. 'We react to each other. What I want, you also want. We feel the same things.'

'No!' she denied in utter panic.

'Yes, Jessica!'

A little roughly, he pulled her back against him. She could feel the length of him imprinted down her spine, he wasn't making any effort to hide the fact that he was now thoroughly aroused.

He began stroking her again, and she closed her eyes blindly, trying to hang on to reality, to deny the storm of emotion that he was whipping up inside of her. How had this happened? *Why* was it happening? Her body shook with a new spasm as his hands inched still lower. For a few seconds her brain refused to function, she was melting, all physical sensation, a mindless creature with no will of her own. Then the spasm receded and she grimly clawed her way back to reality, knowing that she had to figure this out before it hit her again with renewed intensity.

Léon was doing this from need, not love, she told

herself grimly. He wanted something from her, and this
was the only way he could get it. But what was it he
wanted? It was so hard to remember, and that rushing
pleasure was drenching all her nerve-ends again, wave
after wave of it trailing in the wake of Léon's slowly
circling hands. If she didn't remember soon, she was
never going to remember, and then she would be lost,
swallowed up by the chaos he was deliberately causing.

Léon pulled her closer against him, burying his body in
her warmth, his breath harsh against the nape of her
neck.

'*Tu m'enivres*,' he muttered. 'You drive me a little
insane.'

Through the fog that was clouding her brain, she dimly
realised that he was less in control that he would have
liked, that they were both teetering dangerously near the
edge of a bottomless chasm.

With one last despairing effort, she dragged herself
back from the brink, refusing to listen to the aching
protests of her body. For a couple of brief seconds, her
head cleared, she could think with startling clarity. And
all of a sudden she remembered exactly why he was doing
this to her, putting her through this delicious torment.

He was determined that she should agree to marry
him. And not because he loved her, but because he
wanted to get back his inheritance. He was using her!

The memory acted like a cut-out switch. Her body
turned itself off, went blessedly dead. Jessica released a
faint sigh of relief. She was safe—at least, for tonight.

Léon instantly sensed the change in her. With a tiny
growl of frustration, he loosened his grip on her, spun her
round to face him.

She flinched a little as she saw the dark flare of colour
along his cheekbones, the over-bright glitter of his eyes.

'Oh yes, you know very well what you've done to me,

don't you?' he said softly.

'What *I've* done to *you*?' she repeated disbelievingly.
'My God, you really are incredible!'

'Jessica——' he began warningly, but she shook
herself free of him, backed away a couple of steps and
then glared at him.

'Did you have fun tonight?' she demanded sarcastically. 'Were you just starting to congratulate yourself
because your little seduction scene was going so well?
What a shame that it all fell apart at the last moment.'
Her face hardened. 'Do you want to know if I'm going to
marry you, Léon? I'm not. And are you interested in
hearing when you're going to get back your share of the
château? Never!'

And with that, she turned and ran out of the room,
slamming the door so savagely behind her that the entire
château seemed to shudder.

CHAPTER SEVEN

AFTER a sleepless night spent tossing restlessly, her body feeling hot and achy, and strangely empty inside, Jessica crawled out of bed the next morning, then grimaced as she caught sight of her reflection in the mirror.

'All this nervous tension is doing nothing for your looks,' she muttered to herself, staring at her pale, drawn face and dark-rimmed eyes. She found herself remembering the brilliant portrait of her mother which Léon had shown her last night. 'You're never going to be a raving beauty like her,' she added softly, but she found that she didn't really care, it didn't seem important this morning. Anyway, it seemed to Jessica that her mother's beauty hadn't brought her any lasting happiness. Who remembered her now with anything except bitterness and resentment? And even when she had been alive, who had loved her except for André, Léon's father? Jessica supposed that was the price you had to pay for leading a life dedicated to the pursuit of nothing except your own selfish desires.

She turned away from the mirror, and immediately forgot about her mother. Her own problems were much more pressing. What was going to happen when she saw Léon this morning? Come to that, did she even have the nerve to face him again after last night?

Yes, of course she did, she told herself stubbornly. What had happened hadn't been her fault, he was the one who had tried to get his own way by taking things too far. And how cold-blooded could you get? Proposing marriage just so he could get his hands on her share of the château!

With hands that still weren't completely steady, she dabbed make-up on her face until her cheeks glowed and her eyes sparkled, no hint of shadows now. It was marvellous what blusher and eye-shadow could do, she told herself a little cynically. Then she opened her bedroom door and marched downstairs, firmly ignoring the fact that her legs felt distinctly shaky.

When she found there was no sign of Léon in the breakfast-room, she gave a small sigh of relief. It was short-lived, though, because only seconds later Léon's grandmother walked through the door, her black gaze swivelling round to rest on Jessica as if she were something undesirable that the cat had just dragged in.

'You're still here, then?'

'Yes, I am,' agreed Jessica.

'I would have thought a young girl like you would have preferred to return to Paris,' his grandmother remarked pointedly. 'I'm sure that the château must seem extremely dull.'

It certainly wasn't dull last night, Jessica thought a little grimly. She said nothing, though, but merely helped herself to a croissant, although she wasn't at all sure that she could eat it.

'Do you intend to leave before the end of next week?' asked his grandmother.

Jessica sighed. The old lady certainly could be very persistent! And although she had gone to bed last night thinking longingly of the morning, when she could throw her things into a case and skip straight back to Paris, she had been in a very different frame of mind when she had finally got up. She *wasn't* going to run away. These Castillons might have had centuries of practice at getting their own way, but you didn't have to have aristocratic breeding to be tough, she could be as determined as they were. And she had already decided that she wasn't going to let them drive her out.

'No, I'll most certainly be here next week,' she told Léon's grandmother doggedly. '*And* the week after that.' She paused. 'Disappointed?' she asked drily.

To her surprise, the old lady's black eyes simply flashed a little brighter.

'Then you'll be here for the summer ball,' she stated.

'Ball?' echoed Jessica.

'We always hold a ball at the château on Midsummer's Eve,' his grandmother informed her.

'How interesting,' murmured Jessica, without too much enthusiasm. She nibbled at the croissant, then put it down again with a small sigh. Food was definitely out of the question this morning. She raised her head and stared at Léon's grandmother, as always a little intimidated by the old lady's startling resemblance to her grandson. 'Do you know where Léon is this morning?' she asked, with some reluctance. Jessica figured that if she knew where Léon was, she could take steps to avoid him.

'Don't you know?' The old lady's eyes sparkled with a touch of malicious delight. 'He's gone away for a couple of days. On business—or so he said.' She stared hard at Jessica, then added slyly, 'Have the two of you had an argument?'

Jessica stared right back. 'Why on earth should you think that?' she asked, with a coolness that she was far from feeling inside.

'Because he drove off fast and very noisily,' his grandmother answered. 'He only does that when he's in an extremely bad temper about something.'

'Perhaps he simply got out of bed on the wrong side,' suggested Jessica with just a touch of irritability.

Those black eyes glinted brightly again.

'Ah—but whose bed?' remarked his grandmother. Then she turned and swept out of the room before Jessica could think of a suitably cutting reply.

The day didn't seem to improve as it went on. She wandered aimlessly round the château, then the grounds, feeling restless, on edge, and vaguely bad-tempered. She knew that she ought to be feeling relaxed, knowing that Léon had gone and wouldn't be back until the end of the week, but somehow she didn't, and she couldn't really figure out why.

Next morning, she went down to the stables at the back of the château to say hello to the horses and to give a lump of sugar to Isabelle. About to stroll back to the château, she noticed an old bicycle propped up against the stable door. After a couple of turns around the courtyard, to make sure everything was in working order, she sailed off through the gateway; then, on impulse, she started to pedal along the road that led to the Sévignac vineyard.

Claude Castillon was surprised to see her, but made her warmly welcome and insisted that she stay to lunch. After drinking far too much of his delicious wine, she dozed off in the hot afternoon sunshine, only waking up again as the shadows were beginning to lengthen.

Claude was standing there, looking at her and smiling. 'You look about sixteen when you're asleep. Are you sober enough to ride back to the château on that rickety bicycle, or would you like me to drive you?'

'No, I'm fine,' insisted Jessica, jumping to her feet, but she had got up too quickly and for an instant the world spun round, and her head gave an almighty thump. 'Oops,' she murmured, and hurriedly sat down again.

Claude smiled. 'I'll fetch the truck,' he said. 'I won't be long.'

He was back in just a couple of minutes, driving an ancient old pick-up truck. He heaved the bicycle into the back, then opened the door so she could scramble into the front seat beside him.

'Sorry to be such a nuisance,' she apologised.

'You're not a nuisance,' he told her. 'Anyway, Léon would never forgive me if I let you ride back to the château in that state.'

'Léon probably wouldn't care if you let me ride straight under a bus,' Jessica prophesied darkly.

Claude nodded thoughtfully. 'I had heard rumours that there had been—a slight difference of opinion,' he said tactfully.

'Does everyone know everything that happens around here?' she demanded a little balefully.

'I'm afraid so. It's a very small community, and the walls seem to have the proverbial ears.' He paused. 'Do I take it that Léon's proposal of marriage didn't go down too well?'

Ignoring her thumping headache, Jessica sat up very straight. 'Did you think that it would?' she answered tartly.

Claude gave a philosophical shrug. 'I imagine there aren't too many women in France who would turn down a proposal of marriage from Léon. In the circles in which he moves, he is regarded as highly eligible.'

'Well, I turned him down. You didn't honestly think I'd say yes, did you? Come on, Claude, you can give me a truthful opinion. I know that Léon discussed it with you before he even asked me.'

'Ah! And that annoyed you?' Claude asked perceptively. 'That he talked it over with me first?'

'No—yes—oh, I don't know,' she muttered. 'The whole thing's so crazy that it's not worth arguing about. Let's talk about something else.'

'But I haven't answered your question yet,' he persisted. 'You asked me if I thought you'd say yes. And I did.' As her eyebrows shot up in surprise, he went on, 'The idea of a marriage between the two of you isn't really as preposterous as you seem to think. You've a great deal in common when you think about it. You've both had disturbed childhoods, lost one or both parents, had to try and make it on your own. And you each have a strong streak of stubbornness and independence. And now, of course, you also have a shared interest in the château. Looked at from that point of view, marriage seems a rather obvious outcome, don't you think?'

'It certainly doesn't seem at all obvious to me,' retorted Jessica. 'And if you don't mind, I'd rather not talk about it any more.'

'As you wish,' agreed Claude amicably, and he immediately began to discuss the prospects of this year's wine harvest.

Jessica still had a thumping headache when she went to bed that night, and told herself that it was definitely the wine that had caused it, not tension. All the same, she slept badly, and spent the next day roaming around even more restlessly than before, not able to settle to anything, and only picking unenthusiastically at her food.

The following afternoon, Léon returned to the château. Jessica only knew he was back because she was sitting in a window-seat at the time, trying to concentrate on a book and not taking in a single word. A small, bright sports car shot into the courtyard, revved up throatily a couple of times, then fell silent. A second later, the door opened and Léon swung himself out.

Seeing him again gave Jessica an unpleasant jolt. She had forgotten just how tall, how dark he was, how he moved in that supple yet powerful way, somehow dominating any space in which he moved.

She put down her book, jumped to her feet, and hurried out of the room. She didn't want to see him, not just yet. With no real idea where she was heading, she scurried out of one of the back entrances, shot across the terrace, then began to walk very rapidly along the path that wound through the gardens and then led steeply down to the river.

When the glint of water finally showed through the trees ahead, Jessica at last began to slow down. Although she hadn't intentionally headed in this direction, it was as good a place as any to escape from Léon. The only trouble was, she still didn't feel totally safe. Of course, there was no real reason why he should come looking for her, she told herself comfortingly. But just in case he did——

She glanced around, then her gaze rested on the rowing-boats bobbing alongside the jetty. How about the cavern? It would be cool and secluded, the perfect place to sit and try to sort out her confused thoughts. And Léon would never think of looking for her there. He knew she hated boats; it wouldn't occur to him that she would voluntarily get into one and row herself into the Sévignac cavern.

The one big drawback, of course, was that she really *did* dislike boats. All the same, she gritted her teeth and gingerly lowered herself into the nearest one, muttering darkly under her breath as it rocked precariously under her. After she had spent a frustrating few minutes struggling with the oars, the small boat rather erratically began to drift towards the cavern, then she somehow finally manoeuvred it through the narrow entrance.

After she had pulled down the switch that turned on the lights, Jessica sat for a few minutes staring around her with a sense of awe. It was just as magnificent as she remembered it. Then she picked up the oars again and clumsily rowed the boat further inside.

The much cooler air struck her bare arms, and briefly made her shiver. She had no intention of turning back, though; instead she rowed slowly to the very back of the cavern. Then she realised that something was different from last time. The sound of tumbling water had echoed through the cavern on that occasion, like muted underground music. Now she couldn't hear anything except the faint patter of a thin trickle dripping quietly down.

With a small frown, Jessica peered towards the back of the cavern. Where was the waterfall? To her astonishment, she found that it had virtually dried up. Instead of a torrent, just a few rivulets were splashing down the rock-face.

She supposed it had something to do with the rainfall pattern. It hadn't rained since she had come to the château, so the water supply must have simply dried up. The waterfall wouldn't be back at full strength until it rained again.

There was a flat area of dry rock just in front of the waterfall. Tying the boat to a convenient piece of jutting rock, Jessica carefully scrambled out, then went to take a closer look. She couldn't see anything much, though, there were too many dark shadows in this corner of the cavern. Then she remembered Léon had mentioned a box which held the emergency torches. She soon found it. Lifting the lid, she took out one of the two powerful, waterproof torches inside.

Its bright beam easily pierced the black shadows. Jessica aimed it upwards, until she could see the gaping gap in the rock-face high above her, where the water gushed out when the waterfall was in full flood. Then she let the torchlight drift down the glistening rock, feeling a little disappointed that the waterfall wasn't at its spectacular best. She was about to turn away and make her way back to the boat, when something made her stop. Frowning slightly, she shone the torch towards the base of the rock, which was usually hidden by the torrent of water. Why were the shadows so much blacker there? It almost looked like——

It was! A narrow tunnel entrance. But where did it lead? she asked herself with a small twinge of excitement. What if there was another cavern buried deep in the cliff, even bigger and more spectacular than the one she was in now?

'Steady on, Jessica,' she murmured to herself. 'Don't get carried away. It's probably just a dead end.'

But it wouldn't hurt to look. She would be quite safe; the sky outside was clear and blue, it wasn't going to rain so there was no chance of the waterfall suddenly gushing out at full strength again and cutting off her retreat. Anyway, she was only going to poke her head inside, it wouldn't take more than a couple of minutes to see what lay ahead of that narrow gap.

Carefully picking her way over the wet, slippery rock at the base of the waterfall, she reached the gap and shone the torch through. It was definitely a tunnel, she realised with a small thud of her pulses. And it was easily big enough to take her once she had squeezed past the entrance.

Keeping her fingers crossed that the whole thing wouldn't turn out to be a huge disappointment, she took a deep breath, then slipped through the gap and into the tunnel beyond.

It was dry here, although just as cold as it had been in the cavern, perhaps even colder. The torchlight bounced off the walls as she followed the tunnel, and her heart thumped with a mixture of nervousness and excitement. Then the walls suddenly widened, and she found herself

standing in a small cave. She flicked the torchlight over
the walls, then gave a great gasp of total disbelief.

The walls were covered with paintings! A herd of
bison stampeded by on her left, just in front of her a huge
mammoth loomed out of the darkness, while on the other
side of the cave, deer leapt and cavorted over the rock
walls.

Jessica blinked hard, opened her eyes again, and found
the paintings were still there, etched in crude but bright
colours against the pale rock. She knew that prehistoric
cave paintings had been found in other caves in this
region, but to discover them here, at Sévignac—and in
such good condition—it was incredible!

All of a sudden, she found herself remembering Léon's
plans to attract tourists to the area, to try and bring
higher prosperity to the people who lived here. His main
worry had been that the valley couldn't offer any specific
attraction. Well, it looked like that problem had just been
solved! Tourists would come flocking here to marvel at
these paintings.

Jessica wandered around for ages, fascinated by the
primitive vitality of the boldly drawn animals. Then she
found herself wondering if there were still more paintings
further on. Buoyed up with excitement, she set off
eagerly along the tunnel that led out of the far end of the
cave.

The next cave she stumbled into was smaller, but the
paintings here were no less brilliant; more mammoths,
and a herd of horses. Her eyes glued on the walls, she
wandered along, not noticing that the floor of the cave
suddenly dropped away in front of her. An instant later,
her foot found only thin air instead of solid rock floor,
and she went crashing down, plunging straight into a
shallow stream of icy water that trickled through the
centre of the cave.

The impact of the fall made her roll over a couple of
times, so although the water was only very shallow, she
ended up soaked to the skin. Her teeth chattering with
shock and cold, she groped for the torch and sent up a
small prayer of thanks that it was waterproof—and
apparently shockproof! Its powerful beam still cut
through the darkness, and she shakily hauled herself to
her feet, then stood there shivering violently.

'Not very clever,' she muttered to herself. 'Something
tells me it's definitely time to get back to the château.'

She had already been down here much longer than she
had intended, it must be nearly early evening now.
Anyway, she couldn't wait to tell Léon about the
paintings. She had already forgotten how reluctant she
had been to see him earlier.

Trying to forget how freezing cold she was, she turned
round, ready to trudge back along the tunnel to the first
cave. But as she shone the torch round the cave walls,
searching for the entrance, she discovered there wasn't
just one tunnel leading out of the cave, there were three!

As waves of panic began to break over her, she
frantically tried to work out which one would take her
back to the main cavern. Oh damn, if only she hadn't
been so absorbed in those paintings! She would have
noticed those other tunnels when she first came in, she
could have marked the right one and not ended up in this
awful dilemma.

In the end, she plunged down the middle tunnel. If it
was the wrong one, she could just turn back and try one of
the others, she told herself through gritted teeth. Her wet
clothes were clinging icily to her frozen skin now and she
just prayed that she had made the right choice.

It soon became fairly obvious that she hadn't. This
tunnel began to twist and turn, while the other one had
been fairly straight. Fighting back another rush of pure

panic, she swung round and blundered off in the other direction, but the wildly swinging torch in her shaking hand lit up yet more tunnel entrances, it was like trying to find the way out of a maze. Too late, she realised that this place was a virtual catacomb, riddled with tunnels and caves, all interconnected. Once you were lost, it could take for ever to find your way out again.

And she *was* lost. For a while, she refused to admit it, she kept stumbling along doggedly, telling herself over and over that she would soon find the way out, all she had to do was to keep her head and everything would be all right. Only it didn't work out like that. Cold and exhausted, she eventually ground to a complete halt, then slid down into a despairing huddle on the hard ground. 'Time to face the truth, Jessica,' she told herself in a quivering voice. Only a miracle was going to get her out of here.

Thank God the torch was still burning brightly, its powerful beam cutting through the darkness and showing no sign of fading. If she had been in total darkness, she was certain she would have gone quietly insane.

She was afraid to go any further. For all she knew, she could just be going deeper and deeper inside the cliff, getting more and more hopelessly lost. But on the other hand, she couldn't stay where she was. The torch might be shining brightly now but it wouldn't last for ever; she had to try and get out of here before its beam finally went out. The only trouble was, her legs wouldn't seem to work any more, she was so cold, so awfully cold. Even before she had fallen in that stream, she had been aware of the deep chill down here, but with her clothes sodden it was far worse, she was shuddering from head to foot now, and a dangerous lethargy was creeping over her.

She had no idea how long she crouched there in a

shivering huddle, her mind a curious blank, quite incapable of deciding on any definite course of action. When she finally heard the faint echo of a distant voice, she thought she must be talking to herself, perhaps she was finally going a little crazy.

Very slowly, she lifted her head, although it was incredibly difficult, it seemed to weigh a ton. But she could hear the voice again, she *wasn't* imagining it—and it was calling her name. Gathering together the last of her resources, she let out a croaking yell for help.

'Jessica? Jessica! Where the hell are you?'

The voice was Léon's! A great rush of relief swept over her, she tried to struggle to her feet but she couldn't make it, her legs just wouldn't hold her up.

'Jessica, talk to me! It's the only way I'm ever going to find you, by following the sound of your voice.'

He sounded further away again now, and in a sudden panic she shouted his name several times, hearing her own voice echoing round and round as it bounced off the tunnel walls.

'Keep talking,' came Léon's order. 'Your voice will lead me to you.'

Obediently, she began gabbling non-stop, saying the first thing that came into her head. It was a nursery rhyme, one that Aunt Lettie had taught to her. They had recited it together all those years ago when she was young, and life had seemed so uncomplicated. When she had finished it, she launched straight into another nursery rhyme; it was all her cold, tired brain could seem to dredge up.

When the rhyme was over, she paused. She realised she hadn't heard Léon's voice for some time now, and a fresh flare of panic rushed through her. Had she imagined the whole thing? Was she getting delirious?

'Why the hell have you stopped?' demanded Léon, and

she could have cried with relief, for he sounded so near, perhaps only yards away. 'Are you all right?' he called out sharply, his voice suddenly edged with concern. 'Oh, damn! I'm so close but I can't get through to you, these tunnels are like a honeycomb.' There was a short silence, then she heard him give a brief exclamation. 'I think I can see the light from your torch.'

Just seconds later, a dark figure was striding rapidly towards her. With a superhuman effort, Jessica levered herself to her feet; then, with a whimper of relief, she launched herself straight into his arms.

It was sheer bliss to feel the hard warmth of another human body locked close against her own; she just sagged against him limply and didn't want to ever let go of him. She felt his hands slide through her wet hair, then move down and lock around her waist, holding her very, very tight, so tight that she could feel the fast, heavy beat of his heart.

'Dear God, Jessica,' he muttered shakily, 'you could have died down here. Don't you know that?'

She shuddered. Yes, she knew it.

'How did you find me?' she whispered. 'How did you even know I was down here?'

His fingers sank a fraction deeper into her skin, he was hurting her a little now, but she didn't care.

'When you didn't turn up for tea, I wondered where you were,' he told her. 'I asked around, and Gustave said he'd seen you heading towards the river, but that had been a few hours ago and he hadn't seen you since. I went down to the river, to look for you, but there wasn't a sign of you anywhere. I was just about to go back to the château when I noticed one of the boats had gone. I thought it fairly unlikely that you'd gone to the cavern, but I decided I'd better check, just in case you'd got into some kind of trouble.' He drew in a slightly unsteady breath. 'You're rather good at getting into trouble,' he reminded her in a rather hoarse tone.

'Yes, I know,' Jessica said in a very small voice.

'Once I got into the cavern, I saw the boat tied up by the waterfall, but there was no trace of you. I couldn't figure out where you'd gone. I searched the cavern for ages, then I finally found that narrow tunnel entrance behind the waterfall. I couldn't believe you'd been crazy enough to go exploring on your own, but on the other hand, where else could you have gone? Then I reached the second cave, and I saw a trail of wet footprints where someone had obviously recently fallen into the water. That's when I started shouting out—and eventually you answered.'

'Why didn't *you* get lost, the same way I did?' she mumbled.

'I've been marking the tunnel walls as I went along. That's what you should have done, you little idiot,' he told her rather roughly.

'Once I saw those paintings, I couldn't think of anything else,' Jessica confessed. 'Oh, Léon, you *did* see the paintings, didn't you?' For a few seconds, a spark of life shone in her exhausted eyes. 'Weren't they fantastic? They're going to bring the tourists absolutely flooding in, your new scheme will really take off now. You'll probably end up with more tourists than you can cope with, and everyone in Sévignac will make lots and lots of money——' Her voice trailed away as the brief burst of energy abruptly ran out. Léon lifted his head and stared down at her.

'You're soaking wet and icy cold,' he said a little abruptly. 'Get those wet clothes off—no, let me do it,' he added, as her numb fingers began to fumble ineffectually with the buttons. In seconds, he had stripped her down to bra and pants, then his own jacket was around her shoulders. Shivering uncontrollably, she pulled it even tighter around her, but she still couldn't seem to get warm. 'Let's get you out of here,' Léon said decisively. 'Can you walk?'

'I think so,' she said in a voice that suddenly sounded rather slurred. In fact she could only manage it with Léon's arm firmly round her, taking most of her weight.

Afterwards, the journey back to the château was little more than a blur in her memory. She remembered being surprised to find it was dark outside when they finally left the cavern. Then, during the walk up to the château itself, her legs suddenly gave up completely, and with a tiny sound of impatience Léon swung her up into his arms.

'You can't carry me all the way,' she muttered. 'I'm too heavy.'

'You're certainly no lightweight,' he agreed drily. 'But I think I can manage.'

And he did, although he was breathing heavily by the time they finally reached the bedroom. He put her down on the bed, ran his hand over her cold, goose-pimpled skin, and frowned.

'You're still freezing. You'd better have a long soak in a hot bath, it's about the only thing that'll warm you up.'

'No, I'm too tired,' Jessica said sleepily. 'I just want to go to bed. Please, Léon.'

He hesitated, but then gave a brief nod of his head. 'All right.' He slid his jacket from her shoulders, then reached round and unsnapped the catch on her bra.

Jessica's heavy eyes fluttered open. 'What are you doing?'

'Taking off the last of your wet clothes,' he answered patiently. 'You can't go to bed still wearing them.'

'I can undress myself,' she insisted dozily, but she couldn't, even the smallest task seemed totally beyond her now. A brief wave of embarrassment swept over her as Léon efficiently stripped off the last of her damp undies, but she was too exhausted for strong emotions of any kind, she didn't even protest as he scooped her up, then deposited her in the bed.

She instantly burrowed under the quilt, like a small animal seeking warmth and shelter. Deep shivers were still racking her, though, she couldn't seem to raise her body temperature by one single degree. Then she felt something warm beside her, and with a small sigh of relief she instinctively snuggled up to it. It wasn't until she was hovering on the edge of a deep sleep that she finally realised that it was another human body she was curled up against so tightly, as if it were a huge hot water-bottle. She couldn't do anything about it, though, there wasn't even time to feel alarmed at the implications of her discovery. The velvet darkness was already swallowing her up, and she slept soundly and dreamlessly through the rest of the night.

When Jessica next opened her eyes, the room was filled with brilliant sunshine. Yawning hard, she was just about to close her eyes again and snooze for another half-hour when she suddenly remembered everything that had happened yesterday, and she abruptly sat up.

Staring around, she realised what she had been too cold and exhausted to notice last night. This wasn't her room! She was just about to jump out of bed and scurry back to her own bedroom, when she realised something else. She was totally naked under the bedclothes. With a small groan, she dived back under the quilt and was just trying to figure a way out of this predicament when the door opened and Léon strolled in. He was wearing just a short bathrobe, and his hair was damp, as if he had recently showered.

'What are you doing in here?' Jessica snapped nervously.

'This happens to be my room,' he pointed out equably. His black gaze slid over her appreciatively, and she huddled even further under the quilt. 'This is the second time you've woken up in my bed,' he went on reflectively. 'The trouble is, I don't seem to be deriving any real benefit from this very pleasant arrangement. Quite the reverse, in fact. You slept like a log last night, while I——' He shrugged mockingly. 'I had great difficulty in sleeping at all.'

'Serves you right,' Jessica muttered, going bright scarlet as uncomfortably vivid memories drifted back into her mind of the way she had brazenly wrapped herself around him. It was because she had been so cold, she assured herself defensively. And too tired to even know what she was doing. Under normal circumstances, she would never have done any such thing, she was absolutely certain of it.

She glared at him from under lowered lashes. 'Where are my clothes?' Then, realising that she didn't sound particularly grateful, considering that he had probably saved her life yet again, she added rather grudgingly, 'I do appreciate the way you came galloping to my rescue, but I'd like to go back to my own room now. If I stay here, someone might see me, and I wouldn't want them to think—well, that I—that we——'

'That we spent the night together?' Léon finished for her smoothly. 'But we did, *ma chérie.*'

'But nothing happened!' she shot back instantly. 'And please stop calling me that. I am *not* your beloved.'

Something flickered in Léon's eyes, and Jessica instantly felt apprehensive. The man who had showed concern and compassion last night had totally vanished; this morning she was confronted with Léon Castillon,

Comte de Sévignac, the last of a long line of Castillons, all of whom had been accustomed to getting precisely what they wanted. And with a small inner quiver, she remembered that what Léon Castillon wanted was her!

He was staring at her now with extremely disconcerting intensity.

'No, I suppose you're not my beloved,' he finally agreed blandly at last. 'But it might be a little hard to convince Madame Clemenceau of that.'

'Madame Clemenceau?' Jessica repeated warily. 'The housekeeper? Why on earth should she think we're——' she flushed heavily, 'that we're involved with each other,' she finally finished rather lamely.

'Why not say "lovers"?' Léon suggested. 'You're not so prudish that you can't say the word, Jessica. At least, you certainly don't act prudishly when I touch you,' he added, his voice suddenly dropping a couple of tones and taking on a slightly husky quality.

Jessica refused to be side-tracked, even though her skin had started to prickle in a familiar and rather pleasant way.

'What's all this about Madame Clemenceau?' she repeated doggedly.

Léon gave the smallest of shrugs. 'She always brings me a cup of coffee first thing in the morning. Unfortunately,' he went on smoothly, 'this morning I overslept, so I was unable to waylay her and stop her coming into the room.'

'She saw us?' Jessica squeaked in horror. 'In bed together?' She briefly closed her eyes; this was just too much coming on top of everything else. Then they snapped open again, and her violet gaze fixed on him. 'You'd better go and explain the truth to her. Right now!'

'I really don't think that would do much good,' Léon replied, his voice totally calm and his black eyes alight with the satisfied gleam of someone who knows he has the upper hand. 'Madame Clemenceau's very efficient and hard-working, but I'm afraid she has one fault. She's a compulsive gossip. By now, I should think most of Sévignac's been told of the latest interesting event at the château. I regret, my love, that your reputation has been rather badly dented. In fact, I can't see any way you can restore it—except, of course, by agreeing to marry me.'

'You did it on purpose!' Jessica hissed at him, at this moment hating him with an intensity that made her actually shake. 'You knew she'd be coming in here this morning, that she'd see the two of us together. You had it all planned right from the very beginning, that's why you brought me here last night, to *your* room, instead of taking me straight to my own. My God,' she went on savagely, 'you really can be a devious bastard when you want to be, can't you? You twist everything to your own advantage, you don't give a damn about anything or anyone as long as you eventually get your own way. Nothing matters, except what you want!'

The cool mask slid from Léon's face, and suddenly it was a very different man who confronted her: his features dark, his mouth set in a tight, hard line, his black gaze fiercely fixed on her with almost obsessive intensity.

'And I want *you*, Jessica,' he reminded her softly, and there was something in his tone, his abrupt change of mood, that made her nerve-ends crawl with sudden fear. 'I don't think you know quite how much.'

She made a last-ditch effort to drag her quivering nerves back under control.

'Of course I know,' she answered icily. 'You've already made it perfectly plain that you'll do just about anything to get your inheritance back. Even if it means marrying the daughter of the one woman in the world you really hated.'

His eyes glittered warningly. 'You weren't listening to what I was saying.' Rather abruptly, he stood up and paced over to the far side of the room. Then he swung back to face her, and she could almost feel the tension now radiating from his body. 'I never take anything unless it's given willingly,' he told her in a taut voice. 'But I've had a rough night—perhaps only another man could appreciate how rough. So you'd better get out of here before I'm tempted to break that rule.'

'I don't have any clothes,' she reminded him in a biting tone.

He opened a closet, whipped out a bathrobe and tossed it over to her. Then he strode over to the door. 'Don't still be here when I get back,' he advised grimly.

But there was no chance of that! Jessica was out of bed and struggling into the bathrobe as soon as the door slammed shut behind him. Seconds later, she was flying along the corridor to her own room. Safely inside, she paced up and down several times, still blazingly angry at the way he had tricked her. Did he really think he could persuade her to marry him by forcing her into a compromising situation? The man really was incredible!

And he was about to find out that the whole exercise had been totally futile. For once, a Castillon was going to fail to get what he wanted!

CHAPTER EIGHT

JESSICA got over her bad experience in the caves remarkably quickly. She didn't even suffer any nightmares, although she didn't have the slightest inclination to go back for another look at those prehistoric paintings, not just yet.

Her temper didn't die down, though; it kept simmering dangerously near to boiling point over the next couple of days. As far as possible, she ignored Léon, only speaking to him when it was absolutely necessary. Sometimes he looked amused, occasionally she caught him looking unexpectedly grim, but at least he kept his distance and she was grateful for that.

She supposed the sensible thing would have been to have left the château and gone back to Paris, but a deep stubborn streak wouldn't let her, it would have been too much like running away. Anyway, the preparations were well under way now for the ball that would be held at the château on Midsummer's Eve, and Jessica found herself gradually being caught up in the flurry of excitement. It was hard to think straight at the moment, she told herself; she would make some definite decision about the future once the ball was over.

The day before the ball, she was standing at the window, watching a couple of workmen fixing chains of lanterns around the terrace, when she heard the door open behind her. Her heart began to pound rather erratically, but when she turned round, she found it was only Léon's grandmother who had swept into the room.

'I suppose you intend to be at the ball tomorrow?' remarked his grandmother.

'Of course,' replied Jessica, with a touch of defiance. 'Is there any reason why I shouldn't be there?'

His grandmother shrugged. 'I just thought that you might not have anything suitable to wear.'

At that, Jessica's spirits instantly sank half a mile. How on earth could she have overlooked anything so important? The stresses of the last few days must have affected her even more than she had realised.

She flicked mentally through her strictly limited wardrobe, then silently sighed. There wasn't a single thing even remotely suitable for a ball.

'Is there a dress shop in the village?' she asked, although not very optimistically.

'Of course not,' answered his grandmother a little scornfully. 'There's a woman who runs up everyday clothes, but she'd probably collapse with shock if you asked her to make something you could wear to the Sévignac ball.' She paused, then added almost diffidently, 'Of course, there's a whole wardrobe full of clothes in your mother's room. After she died, André locked the doors to her suite and wouldn't let anyone touch a single thing. He turned it into some kind of shrine. As far as I know, everything's still up there.'

'I would have thought Léon would have cleared everything out,' Jessica said with some surprise.

'I dare say he'll get round to it one day. Until now, he's had far more important things to do.'

Jessica stared at the old woman suspiciously. 'Why are you suddenly being so helpful?'

His grandmother stared straight back at her, the coal-black eyes clear and bright. 'Since I can't stop you going to the ball, I can at least make sure you're decently dressed, and don't disgrace the family.' She peered even harder at Jessica. 'I have heard some rather strange rumours,' she went on, rather more abruptly. 'People are saying that my grandson intends to marry you. Is that correct?'

Jessica's head snapped up. 'I can tell you this—*I've* definitely no intention of marrying *him*.'

'Good,' nodded his grandmother. 'Because I certainly wouldn't approve of such a marriage.'

'You do surprise me,' answered Jessica with heavy sarcasm. 'Are you going to tell me why you don't approve?'

'If you like,' responded his grandmother calmly. 'You've no breeding, of course, but my main objection is that you're far too thin. Such skinny hips,' she said disapprovingly. 'Léon needs strong sons, to carry on the name of Castillon. I really don't think you're capable of giving him a healthy heir.'

Jessica was just on the point of exploding when she caught the triumphant glint in the old lady's eyes. Calming down again very rapidly, she stared at Léon's grandmother with dawning understanding.

'Do you know what I think?' she said slowly, at last. 'I think that you enjoy deliberately shocking people. Underneath that stern exterior you're really having a lot of fun. After all, it's pretty quiet here at the château. Not many people come to see you, you haven't got any friends of your own age. So you get your kicks from provoking people, stirring up arguments—it all adds a bit of spice to what's turned into a rather dull life. I was right,' she went on, with fresh certainty, 'you *are* a rude old lady. But you're a rather wicked one as well! And I might as well warn you,' Jessica added, starting to grin broadly now, 'after everything that's happened these past few weeks,

I'm getting to be completely shockproof. You can be as outrageous as you like, it'll just bounce right off me.' She gave a huge, conspiratorial wink. 'I'm off to find a dress to wear at the ball. See you later, *Grand'mère*.'

And as she bounced out of the room, she could have sworn that a very faint smile hovered at the corners of the old lady's thin mouth.

She climbed the stairs to her mother's room, but as she went inside she experienced an odd pang of guilt, for a few moments she almost felt as if she were trespassing. Pushing that daft idea to one side, she walked determinedly over to the wardrobe and pulled open the door. Then she gave a low whistle of sheer amazement.

It was absolutely stuffed with clothes. Silk, satin, crêpe de Chine, silver gauze, hand-embroidered cotton—every single type of material imaginable was there. And a lot of the dresses looked as if they had never been worn. Jessica guessed that her mother had been a compulsive buyer of clothes; it must have all been part of her rather unstable and possessive personality.

The hardest part was choosing an outfit that wasn't too flamboyant. In the end, Jessica chose a silk crêpe dress cut in a twenties style. She was just about to put it to one side when she noticed another dress under a transparent cover. Taking it out, she stared at it for a couple of minutes; then an audacious idea slowly began to blossom inside her head.

Did she have the guts to go through with it? she wondered. Then she remembered how Léon had coolly let the housekeeper walk in on the two of them in bed together. Yes, she did, she told herself fiercely. It wouldn't even start to pay him back for that underhand trick, but he wouldn't like it, he *definitely* wouldn't like it, and a small blow of revenge was better than no revenge at all. She picked up the dress and took it back to her own room, a rather defiant smile on her lips.

Next day, it was chaos at the château as the caterers arrived, exquisite flower arrangements began to fill the rooms, the last of the lanterns were fixed in place, and the musicians tuned up in the main ballroom. Jessica disappeared up to her room late in the afternoon. It was going to take her some time to get ready, and she wanted to get it exactly right. By the time she had finished, the first cars were beginning to roll into the courtyard, Rolls-Royces and Ferraris and Lamborghinis parking alongside rather more commonplace models. People had driven from all over the region to attend the famous Sévignac summer ball.

Léon's authoritative rap on her bedroom door came only minutes later.

'Are you ready?' he enquired, a little impatiently.

Her pulses racing, Jessica walked over and opened the door; then she just stood there so he would get the full effect.

For a few moments, he simply stared at her. Then his black eyes grew absolutely murderous.

'What the hell have you done?' he demanded furiously.

He grabbed hold of her wrist and shoved her back inside the room. As he let go of her again, Jessica swirled round so he could view her from every possible angle.

'Don't you like it?' she challenged. 'I thought it was very—effective.'

'Get it off!' he ordered curtly. 'Right now!'

The light of battle instantly glowed in her violet eyes.

'Why? Because *you* don't like it? Well, *I* think it looks fine, and I've no intention of changing it.'

As she swung away from him, she caught a brief glimpse of her reflection in the full-length mirror on the far side of the bedroom, and for an instant even she was shocked, although she had known perfectly well what she looked like. The likeness was devastating. No wonder Léon looked as if he would like to strangle her.

The dress she had found in the wardrobe—the dress she was now wearing—was the same one her mother had worn when she had posed for that sensual portrait that hung over the fireplace in her bedroom. The exquisite white satin clung tightly to Jessica's breasts, her flat stomach, slithered over her hips before flaring to the full, glistening folds of the skirt. It fitted so well that it could have been made for her. It left her arms and shoulders completely bare, but that didn't matter because she had inherited her mother's flawless skin.

The rest had been easy. Her dark hair had curled naturally into the same style as her mother's, and there had been no problem with the make-up. Working in the theatre had taught her how to apply it quickly and skilfully, using subtle shading to create the exact effect she wanted.

When she had finally finished, she had been quite stunned at the effectiveness of the result. Except for the colour of her eyes, it was like looking at Celestine Castillon all over again. But of course, that had been her intention from the very beginning. And it had worked. Léon looked completely wiped out; even the blaze of anger couldn't fully disguise the underlying and unnatural pallor of his skin.

For an instant, Jessica felt a sharp pang of guilt. It couldn't be very pleasant for him, to be suddenly confronted with the ghost of the woman who had ruined his early adolescence with her subtle torments and perverse teasing. Then her heart hardened again. It was time someone taught Léon Castillon that he couldn't play games with other people's lives and get away with it every time.

He was prowling restlessly round the room now, flinging a brooding glance in her direction every now and then as if he couldn't quite believe what he was seeing. Finally he stopped, and swung round to confront her.

'Are you going to change that dress?'

'Definitely not,' she assured him defiantly.

'In that case, you'd better have the baubles that go with it,' he growled with new venom.

His fingers closed round her wrist, and a second later he yanked her out of the door. She almost had to run to keep up with him as he strode off along the corridor. It was useless to try to get away, her wrist was locked tight within his unrelenting grip. Breathless and suddenly very nervous, she stumbled along beside him and apprehensively wondered where he was taking her.

It didn't take her long to find out. A couple of minutes later he was hauling her through the door to her mother's bedroom, and Jessica found herself face to face with the portrait which she so uncannily resembled.

Léon wasn't looking at the painting, though. Instead he went directly over to the dressing-table, opened a drawer and lifted out a small, ornate box. Whipping open the lid, he took something out, then returned immediately to Jessica's side. As his hands went up to encircle her neck, she gave a small yelp of pure fear.

He smiled at her grimly. 'What do you think I'm going to do? Wring your pretty little neck? Not that I'm not tempted,' he muttered thickly. 'Although perhaps it would be more appropriate to paddle your backside for this childish charade.'

While he had been speaking, his fingers had slipped around her throat, and she felt something cold touch her skin. She turned slightly so she could see her reflection in the mirror, then caught her breath. Around her neck was the heavy gold chain that her mother had worn when the portrait was painted.

'Just one more bauble,' Leon instructed tersely, and he was reaching for her left hand now. A moment later, a ring was slipped on to her third finger.

Jessica glanced down, then caught her breath. It was the other piece of jewellery her mother had been wearing in the portrait, the ring with the dark stone that glinted so brightly.

'It's a black diamond,' Léon told her softly. 'The Sévignac diamond. It's been in my family for generations. It's always given as an engagement ring to the next Comtesse de Sévignac.'

'Then I don't want to wear it,' Jessica said promptly, and she tugged at it furiously, but to her horror she couldn't get it off. 'Léon, it's stuck! You've got to do something, I can't—I *won't* go down to the ball wearing this ring. Everyone will think——'

'What will they think?' prompted Léon silkily. 'That we're engaged?'

'Yes, damn it!' she exploded, furious at this new trick he had played on her.

He regarded her coolly. 'Before I do anything about that ring, let's get one thing straight. Do you still intend to wear that dress to the ball?'

For just an instant, she hesitated. Then her mouth set in a determined line.

'Yes, I do,' she answered stubbornly.

'Then the ring won't be any problem at all,' Léon informed her with unexpected calmness.

'What do you mean, no problem? I can't get it off my finger,' she reminded him angrily.

'No, you can't,' he agreed. 'But that doesn't really matter, because no one's going to see it.'

She stared at him with new wariness. 'What on earth are you talking about?'

His features had somehow changed during these last few seconds: they seemed older, and his eyes were as dark and diamond-hard as the priceless jewel that glittered on her finger.

'Do you know what happens to children who don't know how to behave properly?' he said softly. 'They're locked in their room until they see the error of their ways.'

Jessica's eyes shot wide open. 'Locked in their room? You wouldn't dare——!'

'You think not? And I thought you were beginning to understand me, Jessica. My God,' he went on with sudden vehemence, 'do you really think I'd let you go down to meet my family, my guests, dressed like that?'

'But you can't keep me a prisoner here,' she spluttered. 'It's—it's barbaric!'

'Perhaps it is,' he agreed grimly. 'But when it comes down to it, there's a touch of the primitive in all of us. And when I'm around you, there are times when I definitely don't feel very civilised, Jessica Bryant.'

Her gaze flickered past him, she wondered if she could make a dash for the door. A second later, though, he took a couple of steps back, effectively blocking the doorway.

'People will want to know where I am. They'll come looking for me,' she said a little desperately.

'No, they won't. I'll tell them you're not feeling well, you've got a headache.' A hard, humourless smile touched the taut corners of his mouth. 'That's really rather appropriate. You've certainly given *me* one hell of a headache.'

He swung round and left then, slamming the door shut behind him. And although Jessica was finding it hard to believe that this was really happening, that he would actually have the nerve to lock her in here, a second later she heard the key turn with a loud, echoing click.

For a few minutes, she went a little crazy, pounding furiously on the door and yelling at the top of her voice. Nothing happened, though, no one rushed to her rescue. Her mother's suite of rooms was in a secluded wing of the château, and the walls were thick and soundproof. Eventually, the surge of anger burnt itself out. She gave one last frustrated kick at the door, then moodily turned away.

'He can't keep me locked in here,' she muttered to herself as she paced restlessly across the room. 'He can't!'

But the trouble was, he could. Too late, she realised that Léon didn't give a jot for convention, he made up his own rules as he went along. That was what made him such a dangerous man to cross.

Jessica paused in front of the portrait of her mother, and stared up at it resentfully.

'This is all your fault,' she accused out loud. 'If it hadn't been for you, I'd never have come to the château, I'd never have——'

She stopped abruptly as a massive wave of shock nearly blasted her off her feet. Because what she had been about to say was that she would never have fallen in love with Léon Castillon.

An icy coldness rushed right through her, and her hands began to shake very badly. But that's nonsense, she muttered fiercely to herself through chattering teeth, absolutely appalled by this sudden blaze of revelation. I don't love him, I don't! I *can't*! I'd never do anything so utterly crazy. Just look at the way he's treated me tonight.

But the coldness wouldn't go away, nor would the sheer turmoil of emotion that had suddenly been let loose inside her. A little frantically, she tried to list all the reasons why she shouldn't get emotionally involved with Léon Castillon, and at last, very slowly, she began to get some control over her rioting nerves again. After all, she told herself grimly, she had been in this situation before, imagining herself in love with someone who didn't love her in return. And look how that had turned out! There was no way she was going through all that a second time; she absolutely refused to let it happen.

Still shaking inwardly, Jessica lifted her head and stared resentfully up again at the portrait of her mother. Although a small part of her knew it wasn't fair, she couldn't help bitterly blaming her for this latest disaster. But, after a while, she began to notice little details that she hadn't seen before, each one skilfully but deliberately put there by the unknown artist. A faint twist of discontent in the upper lip of the exquisite mouth; tiny lines of tension between the dark, straight brows; a hint of shadow in the depths of the beautiful eyes.

Jessica at last turned away from the painting. She realised now that it wasn't the portrait of a happy woman. Her mother might have spent her whole life selfishly pursuing her own desires, but it obviously hadn't brought her any peace of mind. And it was funny, but all the old resentment Jessica had always harboured towards her had somehow begun to melt away in these last few minutes. In its place was a strange ache of pity for this woman who had perhaps only been a victim of her own instability.

She wondered why she was suddenly able to see everything in such a new light. Because your own heart's been opened up at last, whispered a small voice inside her head. Jessica instantly shivered, and tried hard to ignore that inner voice, to deny what it was saying. Her heart was untouched! She wasn't going to let anyone— and especially not Léon Castillon—twist and mangle it ever again. She didn't want to know about love, for in her experience it always ended in a lot of pain, and there was never anyone there to help you, you always had to face it on your own. Well, to hell with that, she didn't need it!

She went into the luxurious adjoining bathroom, and scrubbed all the make-up off her face. Then she brushed out her hair until it fell in its usual mop of tousled dark curls. Finally, she took off the white satin dress, tossed it on to a chair, and instead put on a cotton housecoat she found tucked away in a corner of the wardrobe.

Impersonating her mother had been a stupid, infantile idea. Worse than that, it had somehow put a lot of weird notions in her head. And the craziest of all, she told herself firmly, was the idea that she was in love with Léon. In the morning, she would probably laugh herself silly about it. The only snag was, it didn't seem particularly funny right now. In fact, she had never felt less like laughing. And something inside her seemed to hurt, to actually ache, like a bad toothache only worse, much more permanent.

The evening dragged by incredibly slowly. Every now and then the faint echo of music drifted up on the night air. She knew the ball would be in full swing by now, everyone would be having a fantastic time. She could have been down there with them if only she hadn't behaved so stupidly. Jessica sighed, curled up in an armchair and closed her eyes. All she wanted now was for this night to be over. It had turned out so differently from the way she had planned it and, although she hated to admit it, she knew that most of it had been her fault. The only good thing that had come out of it was that, in a strange way, she had started to come to terms with the self-centred, unstable woman who had been her mother.

Occasionally she dozed, sometimes she just sat there, staring into the darkness and trying to make some decisions about her own immediate future. She lost all track of time, and was slightly amazed when the room began to lighten with the first pale glow of dawn.

A few minutes later, the lock suddenly clicked and all her nerves gave a violent jolt. She sat bolt upright in the chair and her eyes widened apprehensively as the door opened, allowing Léon to walk into the room. She noticed that he looked very tired, and his black gaze was suspiciously over-bright, as if he weren't entirely sober.

He leant elegantly against the fireplace, regarding her reflectively.

'I imagine you've had a much quieter night than I've had,' he remarked at length.

'Did the ball go well?' she asked, without much interest.

'It always goes well,' he answered, stifling a yawn. 'Everyone's eaten too much, drunk too much, and I've had a whole string of unmarried daughters paraded in front of me, all of them hoping that they'll be the one to catch my eye.'

'You're so conceited!' Jessica tossed at him in disgust.

'Not conceited, just pragmatic. I've got a title, I'm moderately wealthy, and I'm unmarried. That seems to make me some sort of natural target for every female under fifty. And a handful well over it. Except for you, of course,' he added, that black gaze zeroing in on her with disturbing forcefulness. 'Just lately, you've been treating me as if I've got a serious social disease.'

'Well, you won't have to worry any more about the way I treat you,' muttered Jessica, wishing he would just go away and leave her alone. She felt too vulnerable to cope with all this right now. 'I've made up my mind, I'm going home.'

'Home?' he repeated, a little sharply.

'Back to my apartment in Paris.' She shrugged. 'It's the nearest thing I've got to a home. Once the revue reopens, I'll pick up my dancing career again. I don't suppose we'll see each other again, because I won't be coming back to the château.'

She had thought her anouncement would please him. He certainly didn't look very pleased, though, she noted rather apprehensively.

Léon walked over and kicked the door shut, making her head jerk up nervously. What was he up to now?

'You can't *stop* me going back to Paris,' she warned him with forced defiance. 'Not even you would have the nerve to keep me locked up here indefinitely.'

Léon stared at her for such a long time that she began to feel he was looking right inside her, could read every thought in her head. Oh God, she hoped not! There were several thoughts, several emotions that she definitely didn't want him ever to know about.

'You're right,' he said at last. 'But before you finally run away, I can make sure you don't ever forget me.'

Her pulses began to thump at a dizzying speed.

'What—what exactly do you mean by that?' she challenged, her voice slightly squeaky now with nerves.

He gave a lazy smile. 'Not what you're so obviously thinking. All I intend to give you is one kiss. And that's what I want from you in return, Jessica. One kiss. But it has to be given willingly. I told you once before, I don't ever take anything by force.'

She swallowed hard. What kind of game was he playing this time?

'And what if I refuse?' she somehow managed to get out.

Another relaxed smile played around his flexible mouth. Very casually, he tossed the key to the door into the air, then caught it again. 'I rather think that all the advantages are on my side—don't you?'

It was all depressingly clear. A kiss was the price she would have to pay in order to get out of here. The name of the game this time was blackmail. Of course, he couldn't keep her here for ever, but he could—almost certainly would—leave her locked in here for several more hours if she didn't do exactly what he wanted. And she was determined to return to Paris *today*. Now the decision had been made, she just wanted to leave the château immediately, somehow try and get back to her old way of life, forget all about the Castillons and her inheritance.

But now Léon was telling her she could only do that if she agreed to his demands.

'Just one kiss?' she said at last, hoping he couldn't hear the deep apprehension in her voice.

'Just one,' he confirmed. 'But willingly given,' he reminded her, his voice betraying just a hint of huskiness.

Jessica told herself that she could cope with the situation, that she could easily keep all her emotions battened down until it was over. All she had to do was get through the next minute or so, then she would be free to leave. She took a deep breath, then instinctively braced herself, certain his kiss would be hard, perhaps even savage, since he was obviously determined to leave his mark on her in some way.

She was already standing with her back to the wall, so

she couldn't shrink back any further as Léon slowly walked towards her. Her body stiffened in anticipation of the touch of his hands, but to her surprise he placed one arm on either side of her, his palms flat against the wall, so that not one single part of his body touched hers.

It was several seconds before he moved again. Instead, he stood there simply staring at her, and she wished she knew what he was thinking. It was absolutely impossible to read his mind, though, to know what lay behind those bland eyes, that expressionless face.

Then he finally bent his head, and to her utter astonishment the touch of his lips was butterfly-soft— they caressed, barely touched, tantalisingly gentle, promising so much but giving nothing more than the merest breath of pleasure.

Her violet eyes blinked dazedly as that featherlight kiss at last came to an end. The room was filled with the bright glow of dawn now, and somewhere deep inside her there seemed to be an answering glow, spreading outwards through her entire body, weakening her in subtle ways that she didn't even begin to understand.

'Did you like that?' Léon murmured softly.

Almost against her will, she slowly nodded.

'Would you like me to do it again?'

She meant to say no, but somehow her head didn't get the right message; instead it began nodding again in a faint gesture of assent.

Before she had time to explain that it was all a mistake, she definitely *didn't* want a second kiss, his mouth was exploring hers again, only a little more searchingly, a little more provocatively this time, his tongue flicking almost lazily against her inner lip, leaving a small ripple of heat in its wake.

And this time the kiss didn't come to an end, instead it

just deepened and deepened, sucking away all her will-power, leaving only a fast-growing pleasure to fill the vacuum. His mouth still locked on to hers, Léon shifted his weight slightly: now his hands were no longer pressed against the wall behind her but had set off on a very different journey of exploration. A small sound of protest escaped her, this wasn't meant to be happening, it wasn't part of their bargain. But then his hands moved purposefully onward and she dizzily forgot about her protest, it somehow didn't seem to be important any more.

What was important was the trail of heat that his fingers were leaving behind. The cotton housecoat was already undone, leaving her body open and vulnerable to the touch of his skilful fingers. And his hands seemed to be trailing glowing embers in their wake now, his breathing far less even than it had been before.

It was perfectly clear what he intended, he didn't have to say a single word. One palm warmly cupped the full swell of her breast, his thumb brushing over and over the tautly responsive nipple; then Léon bent his dark head, let his tongue teasingly follow the same path, and the embers burst into tiny, dancing tongues of flame that made her gasp with their bright, scorching heat.

Jessica was absolutely certain he could feel the flames, quite suddenly they both seemed incredibly sensitive to each other's needs and responses. She was vividly aware of the dull heat building up inside him, she didn't need to touch him to know that he was already fully aroused, his usual self-control at a dangerously low ebb.

He briefly lifted his head, his eyes looked curiously troubled.

'I didn't mean to go this far——' he admitted huskily. Then he gave an abrupt shake of his head. 'I suppose it doesn't matter, it's too late now——'

Without another word, he swung her up into his arms, and seconds later she was tossed on to the cool silk covers of the bed. Briefly surfacing back to reality, Jessica wanted to tell him that it should matter, it *did* matter, but he was already fanning the fire back into life again. This time the flames were licking down the long, smooth line of her legs as he slid off the housecoat, and his tongue began exploring with wicked intent. She felt a burst of incandescent heat shoot up her inner thighs and then burn fiercely in a shockingly sensitive part of her body. Oh God, she did love this man! Even through all the chaos churning inside her, that one thought beamed through bright and clear. It was no use denying it any longer, he only had to look at her, touch her, and she was totally helpless.

'I think it's time you made *me* burn a little,' he murmured thickly in her ear, and she didn't need a second invitation, her hands were already greedily reaching for him, as if they were starved for the sensation of his skin against her palms.

The bright glow of the dawn lent vivid colour to his body as she helped him strip off his shirt. As her fingers ran lovingly over the smooth suppleness of his skin, he actually groaned out loud, as if she were branding him. His trousers tossed aside, he returned an instant later to curl the long length of his body against hers, forcing her to acknowledge the strength of his need for her, rubbing himself against her, drawing her hand down and then giving a deep shudder of uncontrollable pleasure as her fingers curled round him. And Jessica could hardly believe this was happening, it was impossible that she was behaving with such abandoned animal delight, and yet she couldn't stop. Her whole body wanted to worship him blindly, there wasn't a single part of him she didn't want to touch and taste.

'Are you going to hate me when this is all over?' muttered Léon. 'But right now, I don't care. And I definitely can't stop——'

But she wasn't really listening, the flames seemed to be eating her up now, just the light brush of his skin was enough to set off a new inferno, and he was touching her now in a hundred different places, his body fitting itself to hers with new and raw urgency. Her arms slid round his back, pulling him even closer, and she felt the strong muscles tense under his hot, damp skin as he fought to hold on to the last dregs of his self-control.

Then without warning, she felt a small spark of fear ignite deep inside her, a primitive female fear of his strength, his maleness, the power he had over her at this moment. Sensing her sudden tension, Léon lifted his head and his black gaze bored down into her.

'I promised you a long time ago that I wouldn't hurt you,' he told her hoarsely. 'Do you think I'd break my promise?'

She stared up at him, panting slightly, her violet eyes huge and dark; then she quietened a little and numbly shook her head.

'Then don't be scared, just let me move like this——' he eased his body slowly down against hers, watching her face intently for any hint of new fear '—and curl your legs round—like so. You see?' he told her softly. 'I'm the one who's trapped. And it's the sweetest trap in the world. Now just relax, Jessica, let go. Don't ever be frightened of me——'

And while he was talking, he was running his hand gently over her, stroking away the last of the tension, leaving her molten under his touch as new flames sprang into life, burning away the last of the fear and leaving her supple, totally responsive. Hardly knowing why she had been so frightened only moments ago, she instinctively reached out to him, and his self-control, already severely stretched, crashed through its limits and he gave a small groan of defeat, his body burying itself in hers, blindly seeking her hot, sweet warmth. Jessica tossed her head, her eyes glazing with pleasure as every movement of his body carried her further along the rhythmic spiral of pleasure that was sweeping her to the very heart of the furnace. She was dimly aware that he was making one last frantic effort to hold on to his self-control, but he failed gloriously and rather spectacularly, and seconds later she felt him plunge into a shuddering riot of pleasure that spilled over into her own body, saturating every nook, every cranny, every nerve-end with the most exquisite pleasure.

Slowly, very slowly, the flames began to retreat; there were just small tongues of warmth licking along all her limbs now, a hot, moist glow somewhere deep inside her. She heard Léon's breathing haltingly return to normal, then he raised himself on one elbow and trailed one finger down the length of her damp body, letting his hand finally rest gently on the soft swell of her thigh.

'And all from just one kiss,' he murmured, and she heard the echo of laughter and a faint hint of astonishment in his voice. He stared at her a little longer; then he gave an oddly rueful shake of his head and coiled up beside her, his arm locking itself around her waist, his face buried in her tousled hair.

'Sorry,' came his sleepy mutter. 'I know it's not very polite, but I don't think I can stay awake a second longer. We'll talk later—there's so much I want to say to you——'

His voice trailed away, and Jessica felt him relax totally as he slid into a deep, heavy sleep. She knew that she couldn't sleep, though, she was suddenly unexpectedly awake and alert, her body oddly tense instead of languid and relaxed. The sweat dried on her skin, and a cool chill gradually crept over her. The magic was fading away now, she couldn't seem to hold on to it, hard though she tried. And in its place came a lot of things she didn't want to remember. But she *did* remember them—and her skin grew even colder.

'What the hell have you done, Jessica?' she muttered to herself in growing horror as reality started to flood over her with appalling clarity. The one man in the world she shouldn't have got involved with, and she had let him make love to her! All he'd had to do was touch her, and she had been a complete push-over. He must have been laughing to himself at how easy it had been. He had said they would talk when he woke up, and she already knew precisely what he intended to talk about—their marriage. Now that he had got her into bed, he was confident the rest would be easy, that she would agree to absolutely anything. At last he would get what he had wanted all along: his inheritance intact, secured through his marriage to silly little Jessica Bryant who had ended up like all the other women there must have been in his life—head over heels in love with him, and flat on her back in his bed!

A little grimly, she struggled free of his imprisoning arm. Léon gave a grunt of protest, but didn't wake up, and seconds later she was sitting on the edge of the bed and staring down at him. For a moment, something inside her seemed to melt: she had an almost uncontrollable craving to forget about everything else and just crawl back into his arms.

Then her head snapped up, her spine became rigid. No more one-sided affairs, she reminded herself fiercely. And she had to face the painful fact that this could never turn into anything else. In all the torrent of physical emotion that had passed between them, Léon hadn't spoken a single word of love. As far as she knew, they didn't even exist in his vocabulary. What had he told her? 'I've never been in love in my life, and I don't intend to be in the future.' Well, that was pretty clear. At least she didn't have any illusions about their relationship.

If she left now, it would hurt like hell. But if she stayed, it was going to be a lot more painful and soul-destroying in the future. She might not even get out of it in one piece.

Be sensible, Jessica, she told herself with grim determination. But even so, it was several more minutes before she finally summoned up enough strength to get to her feet, moving almost like a zombie, walking silently out of the room on legs that didn't want to carry her anywhere except straight back to that bed, and to the man sprawled out on it.

After reaching her own room, it took her only minutes to dress and pack. At the last moment, she remembered the ring on her left hand, with its priceless black diamond. Last night, it had been stuck firmly on her finger. This morning, she gave it a small tug and it came off immediately. It was almost like an omen, she told herself silently and a little bitterly. She put the ring carefully on the dressing-table, picked up her case and moved steadily towards the door.

The château seemed strangely silent: the party guests had all departed and the clearing up wouldn't start until later, when everyone had had a chance to sleep off last night's revels. Jessica walked through the empty corridors, let herself out through the front entrance, then crossed the cobbled courtyard. She didn't once look back, she didn't want to see the familiar silhouette of the château proudly outlined against the soft blue of the early morning sky, she wouldn't let herself think of the man who was sleeping peacefully within its walls.

Ignoring the unfamiliar, languid tiredness of her body, she passed through the gateway, then kept steadily going, part of her already feeling as if it had just shrivelled up and died.

CHAPTER NINE

IF anyone had asked her, Jessica couldn't have told them how she had got back to Paris. She had vague memories of buses, of trains, even of hitch-hiking. When she finally reached her apartment, she was totally wiped out; she simply flopped on to the bed and slept until late the next day.

When she woke up, she felt worse, not better. And that seemed to set the pattern for the days that followed. It didn't get any easier, not by one little jot. The days seemed long, the nights endless, and everything was touched with a curious colourlessness; the whole world seemed to have turned to a depressing shade of grey. And she hurt, actually *hurt*, as if her mental misery had translated itself into a hundred and one different aches and pains, each one a small torment.

For the first few days, she tensely waited to see if Léon would come after her. She prayed that he wouldn't, but still rushed to the window every time a car drew up outside, and her nerves jangled mercilessly whenever the phone rang in the hallway below.

But when a call finally did come through for her, it wasn't Léon on the other end, but Maggie.

'I heard you were back in Paris,' Maggie said cheerfully. 'I thought I'd better give you a ring, to let you know the revue's opening again next week.'

'Revue?' echoed Jessica dully.

'The place where we work. Remember?' prompted Maggie. 'The damage from the fire wasn't as bad as they first thought. They've managed to get everything fixed up, and there'll be a couple of rehearsals at the end of this week, just to run through the main routines.' She paused. 'Jessica? Are you still there?'

'Yes, I'm here,' Jessica confirmed, after a moment's hesitation.

'I'll see you at the theatre, then. I've got to rush, I met a gorgeous new bloke last week, and he's taking me out to lunch. 'Bye, Jess.'

Yet when the time came, Jessica very nearly didn't bother to go to the theatre. At the last minute she forced herself to drag along; anything was better than sitting in her apartment, going quietly out of her mind. And by the end of the rehearsal, she was so stiff and aching that, for the first time in ages, she actually forgot about Léon for a few minutes.

Maggie grinned when she saw her.

'Someone hasn't been doing their daily work-out,' she said a little gleefully.

Jessica groaned. 'You're right. Every muscle feels as if it's just been pummelled by a sadist.'

'By the way, how did it work out with that stepbrother of yours?' asked Maggie casually. 'His father left you some sort of inheritance, didn't he?'

'A half-share in a château,' Jessica said, her voice suddenly tight. 'But I shan't be going back, and I don't suppose I'll be seeing Léon—my stepbrother—again.'

'Pity,' commented Maggie. 'I only caught a brief glimpse of him, but he looked really dishy.' She picked up her bag. 'See you next week.' Then she grinned. 'You'd better spend the weekend soaking in the bath. It's the only way you're going to be in a fit state for opening night next week.'

Ignoring Maggie's advice and her own aches and pains, Jessica worked out doggedly for the next couple of days, trying to get her body back into its usual supple state. By the time opening night came round, she could bend and twist without groaning, and once she was back in the grinding routine again, sharing the overcrowded, noisy dressing-room, dashing up for the next costume change and then rushing back down to the stage for the next routine, life slowly took on some semblance of normality. And yet it wasn't the same as it had been before: the spark of excitement, of enthusiasm had gone, all too often the world still seemed that same dull shade of grey that it had been ever since she had run away from the Château de Sévignac.

It was a couple of weeks later that there was a tap on the dressing-room door after the last performance.

'Flowers for Mademoiselle Bryant,' called a voice from outside.

A ripple of excitement ran through the other girls. Although the leading dancers often got flowers, it was fairly rare for any to find their way up to the dressing-rooms of the show dancers.

'Well, open the door someone,' Maggie said practically, at last. 'Let's take a look at these flowers, and find out who's sent them.'

Sue was nearest to the door. She pulled it open, then whistled expressively.

'Wow! They're gorgeous!'

The others had all started to cluster around the doorway, so Jessica couldn't even see the flowers. She didn't want to, though, their delicate perfume was already drifting over to her and even that was somehow making her head whirl dizzily.

'Hey, whose flowers are they?' demanded Maggie a few seconds later. 'Let Jessica at least have a look at them.'

The rest of the girls reluctantly drew back, leaving Jessica with a clear view of a huge basket of white, perfect carnations. Every bloom was exquisite, their scent subtle and yet intoxicating.

'That's funny, there's no card,' frowned Maggie as she peered into the basket. 'They must have forgotten to put one in.'

'Now you won't know who your secret admirer is,' teased Sue.

Still feeling oddly light-headed, Jessica slowly got up and walked over to the basket of flowers. Then, as if she couldn't help herself, she reached out and let her fingertips lightly touch the frilled petals of the snow-white carnations.

Instantly, a queer tingle ran through her wrist, then it shot right up her arm, scorching through her nerve-ends like a silent message from the man who had sent the flowers. Snatching back her hand as if it had just been burnt, she stared at the carnations in bewilderment. Why had he sent them? What game was he playing now? Whatever it was, she didn't want to know about it, and her expression suddenly hardened.

'I don't want them,' she said abruptly. 'Someone else can have them.'

'Don't be daft,' said Maggie reasonably. 'They're yours, no one else is going to take them.'

'I don't want them,' she repeated stubbornly, and she turned her back on them.

But when the rest of the girls finally left, none of them would take the flowers with them. Jessica knew she couldn't leave them here, the dressing-room was already hopelessly cluttered, there just wasn't space for a large basket of flowers. And for some reason that she couldn't explain to herself, she couldn't bring herself to just throw them away.

And so she found herself trudging through the dark streets reluctantly toting the basket of carnations. She refused to let herself think about Léon's reasons for sending the flowers. Right now, she felt too confused, too vulnerable. She would think about it in the morning. Perhaps her head would feel clearer after a few hours' sleep—if she ever managed to get any sleep, she thought to herself rather grimly. Just lately, she had been plagued by bad bouts of insomnia.

She reached her apartment and opened the door, but in the instant before she switched on the light she had a sharp presentiment of danger. Then the bright electric glow flooded the room, and her body seemed to freeze as she saw the tall, dark figure standing by the window.

His face was more drawn than she remembered it. Yet nothing else seemed to have changed, not the dark hair, the vivid scar, or the intense black gaze.

'How did you get in?' she somehow managed to ask in a stiff, expressionless voice.

Léon shrugged lightly. 'It wasn't difficult. I told the *concierge* that I was your stepbrother, and you were expecting me.'

With some difficulty, Jessica tore her gaze away from his face and stubbornly ignored the suffocatingly fast pounding of her heart. 'Why are you here?'

'I wanted to know what you would do with my flowers, whether you would keep them or throw them away. I see that you've kept them,' he added softly yet challengingly.

'Don't read anything into that!' she snapped back. 'I just couldn't bear to see such beautiful flowers dumped into a bin, that's all.'

'And the fact that I'd sent them didn't have anything to do with it?'

'Certainly not,' she retorted instantly. 'They could have been sent by the hunchback of Notre-Dame, for all I care.'

'Liar,' he said lazily.

There was something about his tone that made a rash of goose-pimples spring up all over her body.

'What did you call me?' Jessica said through gritted teeth.

'Liar,' he repeated, almost cheerfully. 'If you hated me—really hated me—you'd have tossed those flowers out without giving it a second thought. So now we've established that you don't hate me, let's get something else sorted out. Why did you run away from the Château de Sévignac?'

'I'd have thought that was perfectly obvious,' she told him coldly.

'Obvious or not, I still think you should tell me about it,' he answered calmly. 'If it had all turned out rather disastrously when we went to bed together, I could have understood it. But it wasn't a disaster, was it, Jessica?' he reminded her in a velvet-smooth voice.

That was something she didn't want to think about, *wouldn't* think about.

'I just want you to get out of here,' she muttered. 'We haven't anything more to say to each other.'

To her surprise, he didn't react angrily, he just kept studying her in a rather unnervingly thoughtful manner. 'I'm going nowhere until you've told me why you ran out on me,' he said finally. 'I think I know the answer, but I want to hear you actually say it.' His gaze ran over her searchingly, she felt as if he was taking her apart and not bothering to put her back together again. 'And don't spin me a line about incompatibility,' he went on in that same astonishingly calm voice. 'We were fantastic in bed together, and I know enough about women to know that it was as good for you as it was for me.'

She stared at him in disbelief. He made the whole thing sound like a damned talent contest!

'Sure, we were good in bed. But that was all!'

He took a step forward. 'No, that was *not* all. You're not that kind of woman, Jessica. You don't jump into bed with someone just because you feel like it, there's got to be something more, something deeply personal behind it.'

This was getting on to highly dangerous ground, and quite suddenly she didn't want it to go any further. She felt too defenceless, she was only going to end up even more badly hurt than before.

'I wasn't talking about me, I was talking about you,' she argued a little desperately. 'Right from the very beginning, you made it perfectly clear what your position was. You didn't love me, you didn't want me, you just wanted to marry me to get your inheritance back again!'

'I never said I didn't want you,' he pointed out. 'In fact, I thought I'd made it rather obvious that I did.'

'All right,' she amended, 'so you enjoyed going to bed with me. But that's no basis for a relationship, Léon. At least, not any kind of relationship that I'd be interested in.'

His face altered, and he sat down rather heavily in a chair on the far side of the room.

'I seem to have gone about this entire affair with a total lack of finesse,' he said drily. 'My only excuse is that I haven't had a lot of practice at this sort of situation.'

Jessica's eyebrows shot up. 'Come on,' she said derisively, 'who do you think you're kidding? Do you seriously expect me to believe that you're naïve where women are concerned?'

His eyes seemed to go a shade deeper. 'Oh no, not naïve,' he confirmed quietly. He raised his head. 'Do you want to know what it's been like for me so far? I'll tell you. It's going to sound arrogant, but I can't help that, from now on you're getting the truth, like it or not.' He paused then went on, 'When you've got a title and a reputation for being able to make money fairly consistently, it's surprising how easy it is to find all the women you want. Most of the time, I'd click my fingers and they'd come running. And even if they didn't, it never bothered me, none of them were anything more to me than just friends. Intimate friends, usually, I'll grant you that—but just friends, all the same. Then I clicked my fingers at you, and you were totally unimpressed. Rather to my surprise, I found I didn't like that. Then I went one step further and offered you marriage, the one thing every woman I've ever been involved with has wanted from me. You turned me down flat and I liked that even less, so I tried to work out why I found your rejection so disturbing. I couldn't make any sense of it, though, it remained a total mystery.'

'And have you finally managed to work it out?' she enquired a little sarcastically.

He relaxed back in the chair, and studied her thoughtfully.

'Oh yes, I've worked it out. But I don't think you have yet.'

Jessica gave an exaggerated sigh. 'Léon, it's late and I'm not in the mood for guessing games. Just tell me why you're here, then get out. I'm tired, and I've got to be up early in the morning.'

'Why am I here?' he repeated, his black eyebrows lifting slightly. 'To persuade you to come back to the Château de Sévignac, of course.'

'I don't believe this,' she muttered, shaking her head. 'I'd like to hear one good reason why I should ever want to go back to the château.'

Léon levered himself to his feet. 'I can give you several reasons,' he told her, after a brief pause. 'For a start, my grandmother misses you. She hasn't had a decent argument with anyone since you left.'

'If she's that desperate for amusement, I'll ring her up and she can fling insults at me over the phone,' retorted Jessica.

Unexpectedly, Léon grinned. 'I always knew that the two of you would eventually get on rather well together. But you want another reason for coming back? How about those cave paintings you discovered? I've had an expert in to look at them, and he nearly exploded with excitement when he saw them! He reckons they could turn out to be one of the most important discoveries of prehistoric art this century. The tourists should come streaming in once we open the caves to the public. We'll have to divert the waterfall, of course; we can't have people getting drenched every time they go into the caves. And we'll need guides, and some kind of route-marking inside the tunnels. One person getting lost inside those caves is one person too many. Particularly when that person happened to be you,' he added, his face briefly darkening.

'I still don't see what any of this has got to do with me,' Jessica argued. 'I suppose it's exciting——'

'Damn it, of course it's exciting!' he interrupted, his black eyes blazingly bright now. 'But it needs someone to organise the whole thing, make sure that the people of Sévignac get their fair share of all the money this project's going to bring in.'

'I'm a dancer, not an administrator,' she reminded him, firmly blocking out the dazzling possibilities he was starting to conjure up. Oh God, if only he would go! She wasn't sure how much more of this she could take.

'You can be anything you want to be,' he said, after a short pause. 'You've got brains, you've got enthusiasm, and you've got a feeling for Sévignac and the people who live there. And I don't think you're really committed to a full-time dancing career, Jessica. Did you miss being in the revue, all the time you were at the château?'

'Of course,' she said instantly, but she was lying. She hadn't given it a passing thought, she hadn't even bothered to keep up her daily work-out which kept her dancer's muscles in trim.

Léon prowled restlessly towards her, finally coming to a halt a couple of feet in front of her, his black brows drawing together in a frustrated frown.

'All right,' he growled reluctantly. 'Do you know the real reason why you've got to come back to the château? It's because I'm in love with you, and I don't know how the hell I'm going to get through the rest of my life if you're not right there beside me!'

All the strength drained right out of Jessica's legs, and she sat down rather abruptly on the chair just behind her.

'I don't—I don't believe you,' she stuttered, her violet eyes absolutely huge with shock.

Léon ran his fingers edgily through his hair.

'I didn't think you would,' he admitted, with a touch of resignation. 'To be perfectly truthful, I didn't believe it either, not at first. That's why I didn't come after you straight away when you left the château. I needed to get it straightened out in my own head first, know exactly what it was I was offering you. And I thought you might need a little breathing space, as well. I was pretty sure you were in love with me.' He grinned unexpectedly. 'No one behaves like that in bed, Jessica, unless they're fond— *very* fond—of the man they're with. But when you went haring off to Paris, I thought you might be feeling as confused as I was, that you needed some time to sort it all out in your own mind. And of course,' he added reflectively, 'they do say that absence makes the heart grow fonder.' He stared down at her with eyes that suddenly weren't unreadable any longer, but blazing fiercely with a quite unmistakable emotion. 'Have you grown any fonder of me since you last saw me?' he asked a little huskily.

Jessica discovered that she was trembling quite violently. And inside her head, there seemed to be nothing except total chaos as she rather desperately tried to come to terms with his incredible confession. What exactly was he telling her? That this *wasn't* a one-sided affair? That he loved her, wanted her, every bit as intensely as she loved him? But that was impossible, she just couldn't believe it, she couldn't!

Léon was watching her now through dark, narrowed eyes.

'You think I'm lying?' he challenged softly. 'Exactly what do I have to do to convince you?'

'I—I don't know,' she whispered.

He came a little nearer.

'Do you remember the first time you touched me?' he asked, never letting his black gaze leave her face for a single instant. 'Remember how it felt?' He held out his hand, palm upwards. 'Want to try it again?' he invited a little huskily.

Numbly, she shook her head.

'Don't be a coward, Jessica. Give me your hand.'

And somehow her fingers were creeping towards his, his entire body seemed to act like some kind of magnet. Seconds later, her palm was hovering over his, and she actually gasped out loud as their skin finally came into contact.

Tiny prickles of response ran sharply along all her nerve-ends, her palm seemed to be growing extraordinarily hot, and once again she had the unnerving sensation that their hands were becoming welded together. And he had moved even closer now, still touching her only with the palm of his hand, but bending his head until his lips hovered tantalisingly near, making her sway forward a little as his strong body magnetism kept working, dragging her still closer.

Then their lips were actually touching, his mouth moving lovingly over hers, exploring, caressing, forcing her to accept the strength of his feelings for her.

When he finally released her, she stared up at him dizzily and discovered that he was smiling.

'I think you're finally beginning to accept that I really do love you,' he said with some satisfaction. 'Although a kiss can often cause a lot more problems than it solves,' he reminded her teasingly. 'Remember what happened last time I kissed you?'

Jessica instantly went a glowing shade of scarlet. She certainly did!

'On the other hand,' Léon went on, 'we still haven't solved all our problems. We've established that I love you, I'm pretty certain that you love me, even if you *are* too stubborn to admit it to my face. So the next question is, where do we go from here?'

'I don't know,' she mumbled, still feeling totally dazed. 'Do you—do you still want to marry me?'

Léon looked at her with loving exasperation.

'I've never stopped wanting to marry you. It's just that my motives have changed—and for the better, I hope,' he added drily. 'I don't give a damn about the château, about my inheritance any more. They suddenly stopped being important. It's *you* I want, Jessica. But despite what I said earlier, I don't want to bulldoze you into giving up your dancing career; you'd only end up hating me if I wrenched you away from it by force.'

Her violet eyes were soft and dark as she looked up at him. 'I can't think of anything on this earth that could make me hate you,' she admitted huskily. 'I love you, Léon. These past few weeks have been sheer hell, thinking I was never going to see you again.'

'So how are we going to make this marriage work? What compromises are we going to have to make?' He gave a small gesture of frustration. 'I'm going to have to spend a lot of time at the château in order to get this new tourist scheme off the ground. And if you're here in Paris, we're only going to be able to spend an odd day, perhaps an occasional weekend together. I'm not sure I can cope with that, Jessica,' he went on a little thickly, one hand running gently but possessively over her shoulder, down one arm, finally coming to rest against the soft underswell of her breast.

She gave a small shiver of pleasure at his familiar touch. 'Perhaps you won't have to cope with it,' she told him unsteadily. 'Dancing only played such a big part in my life because there was nothing else to compete with it. I realise that now, I can see a lot of things much more clearly. Since I came back to Paris, it hasn't been the same—dancing in the revue seemed like just another job of work. I didn't even enjoy it very much, it was just a way of filling in a lot of empty hours.'

Léon stared at her a little disbelievingly. 'You'd be willing to give it up?'

She nibbled her underlip slightly anxiously. 'Er—as a matter of fact, I might not even have a lot of choice. It might be giving me up.'

'What on earth are you talking about?'

Jessica fidgeted around for several seconds before finally answering him.

'I think—I'm not sure——' she said carefully, '—but I think I might be pregnant.'

For an instant, all the colour left his face, and his hand, which had been busy familiarising itself all over again with the rich curves of her body, became very still.

'Léon?' she said rather anxiously.

'How long have you known?' he asked abruptly.

'The possibility occurred to me a couple of days ago. But I didn't even want to think about it, I shoved it right to the back of my mind and just tried to forget about it. Anyway, I told you, I'm not certain. I might just be a few days late. It happens sometimes.' She stared at him uneasily. 'If I'm not wrong—if it's definite—how do you feel about it?'

He drew in a long, unsteady breath.

'How do I feel about it?' he repeated slowly at last. 'I think it's incredibly, totally, bloody marvellous!'

Jessica sagged slightly with relief. 'I wasn't sure how you'd take it, if you'd be pleased or not.'

'Do you want to know just how pleased I am?' he demanded. 'If it does turn out to be a false alarm, I'll take you straight back to bed and keep you there until it *is* definite.'

She grinned with some satisfaction 'That could take months.'

'I sincerely hope that it does,' he told her throatily.

Jessica's eyes danced. 'It looks as if I might finally win your grandmother's approval,' she teased. 'At this rate, we shouldn't have any trouble turning out half a dozen Castillon heirs. She'll just have to take back her remarks about my skinny hips.'

His hand slid appreciatively over the taut swell of her buttocks. 'You're not skinny,' he told her, 'you're absolutely perfect.' His eyes glittered a little wickedly as his fingers pressed more firmly into her highly responsive flesh. 'How traditional a bride are you going to turn out to be?'

'What do you mean?' asked Jessica rather breathlessly, finding it distinctly hard to think straight while he was subjecting her to those lethally pleasurable caresses.

'Are you going to make me wait until our wedding night before you let me back into your bed again?'

'I think—perhaps it would be best,' she said with some reluctance after several moments' thought. 'Léon, don't do that!' Then she sighed softly. 'Oh yes, please do it—and again——'

The touch of his fingers turned into an aching trail of pleasure, and it was several minutes before he gave a frustrated grunt, then pushed her away from him.

'Enough, Jessica! My self-control crashes to an all-time low every time I come near you, and right now I'm just about to fall apart inside with wanting you. I'm warning you, I intend to marry you just as soon as I can arrange it.'

'I don't care how soon it is,' she assured him huskily.

'And you won't mind living at the château?'

'I'd live in a hut in the middle of a field, as long as you were there with me.' Then she raised her head, and a brief glimmer of her old determination shone in her violet eyes. 'But I don't intend to sit around all day playing at being the gracious chatelaine. Pregnant or not, I want to get involved in this tourist scheme of yours. After all, I was the one who found those cave paintings,' she reminded him, 'so, in a way, they're my baby.' Then she grinned ruefully. 'Sorry, unfortunate choice of words. But you know what I mean.'

'Yes, I know. And it's all right, sweetheart, I don't want to shut you out of anything, keep you locked away in some ivory tower.' Léon's mouth curved into an answering smile. 'In the past, you've accused me of being barbaric and medieval, but you'll find I'm fairly up-to-date in a lot of ways. For instance, I believe that marriage should be a partnership. You can get as involved as you like in the development of those caves as a prime tourist attraction—just as long as you leave plenty of free time for some equally important things,' he added in a very different tone of voice.

Jessica shot him a demure look from under lowered lashes.

'What kind of things?' she asked innocently.

He growled softly. 'You know damned well!'

'I seem to have forgotten. Perhaps you had better—remind me,' she suggested delicately.

'But you said——' He stopped abruptly, and glared at her with mock exasperation. 'Are you playing games with me?'

'No games,' she said, relenting. 'This is for real, Léon.' Her voice wasn't entirely steady now. 'I changed my mind,' she went on with just a touch of shyness. 'Female's prerogative.'

He gave a small groan as she slid her arms around his neck, his hands came up and locked on to her, holding her prisoner.

'I love you, I need you, Jessica. And right now, I'm pretty vulnerable where you're concerned, so make sure you know what you're doing, what you want, or you could get us into a situation where you won't have a choice any more.'

Her grip on him tightened. 'I know exactly what I want,' she whispered. 'I want *you*. For ever and a day. Even longer, if it's possible.'

'We'll make it possible,' he assured her lovingly. Then he gave a small groan, bent his head, kissed her with a deep but gentle hunger, and Jessica closed her eyes and let the world dissolve into a swirling pool of endless delight.

ATTRACTIVE, SPACE SAVING BOOK RACK

Display your most prized novels on this handsome and sturdy book rack. The hand-rubbed walnut finish will blend into your library decor with quiet elegance, providing a practical organizer for your favorite hard-or soft-covered books.

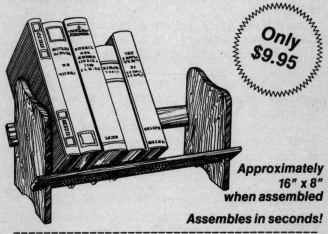

Only $9.95

Approximately 16" x 8" when assembled

Assembles in seconds!

To order, rush your name, address and zip code, along with a check or money order for $10.70* ($9.95 plus 75¢ postage and handling) payable to *Harlequin Reader Service*:

Harlequin Reader Service
Book Rack Offer
901 Fuhrmann Blvd.
P.O. Box 1396
Buffalo, NY 14269-1396

Offer not available in Canada.

BKR-1A

*New York and Iowa residents add appropriate sales tax.

Harlequin Intrigue
Adopts a New Cover Story!

**We are proud to present to you
the new Harlequin Intrigue cover design.**

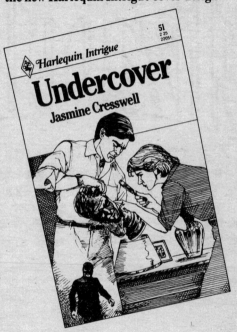

Look for two exciting new stories each month, which mix a contemporary, sophisticated romance with the surprising twists and turns of a puzzler . . . romance with "something more."

HARLEQUIN SIGNATURE EDITION

CAROLE MORTIMER

JUST ONE NIGHT

Hawk Sinclair—Texas millionaire and owner of the exclusive Sinclair hotels, determined to protect his son's inheritance. Leonie Spencer—desperate to protect her sister's happiness.

They were together for just one night.
The night their daughter was conceived.

Blackmail, kidnapping and attempted murder add suspense to passion in this exciting bestseller.

The success story of Carole Mortimer continues with *Just One Night*, a captivating romance from the author of the bestselling novels, *Gypsy* and *Merlyn's Magic*.

**Available in March
wherever paperbacks are sold.**

WTCH-1